GETTING INTO THE GAME

GETTING INTO

FRANKLIN WATTS
A DIVISION OF GROLIER PUBLISHING
NEW YORK   LONDON   HONG KONG   SYDNEY
DANBURY, CONNECTICUT

THE GAME

WOMEN AND SPORTS

BY JUDITH E. GREENBERG

For Marsha DeMunter, a friend who knows how to go the distance, and for every coach who has given of her or his time to
help young girls begin to feel the power to play and to compete
and the spirit to win or lose.

Frontispiece: The 50-yard dash for women at a 1911 company picnic

Photographs ©: Allsport USA: 119 (Sylvain Cazenave/Agence Vandystadt), 83 (Brain Drake),
105 (Mike Powell), 134 (Rick Stewart); Allsport/Hulton Deutsch: 75, 77, 150; AP/Wide World
Photos: 47, 81, 124; Brown University, University Relations Photo Library: 13, 92 (John
Forasté); Christine Osinski: 93; Comstock: 147 (Art Gingert), 96 (Sven Martson), 10; Corbis-
Bettmann: 2, 3, 6, 25, 36, 39; David Silverman/Brown University: 69; ESPN: 142 (John Atash-
ian); North Wind Picture Archives: 21; Packer Collegiate Institute, Brooklyn, NY: 70;
Reuters/Corbis-Bettmann: 89, 100, 121, 127, 130; Smith College Archives: 31, UPI/Corbis-
Bettmann: 1, 50, 52, 57, 73, 85, 87, 115.

Library of Congress Cataloging-in-Publication Data:

Greenberg, Judith E.
        Getting into the game: women and sports / by Judith E. Greenberg.
            cm.—(Women then—women now)
        Includes bibliographical references (p.) and index.
        ISBN 0-531-11329-9
        1. Sports for women—United States—History. 2. Sports—Sex differences.
        3. Sports—Sociological aspects. 4. Women athletes—Biography. I. Title. II. Series.
GV709.G64   1997
796'.0194—dc20   96-38706
                                                                                   CIP

CONTENTS

ACKNOWLEDGMENTS

*T*ucked away in a small brick building in the middle of a large park in East Meadow, New York, is the Women's Sports Foundation. This foundation is a nonprofit educational organization dedicated to promoting and enhancing the sports and fitness experience for all girls and women. This organization deserves credit for its tireless efforts to introduce young girls to the benefits of all sports and for its continuing recognition of outstanding women athletes. I wish to thank the staff and interns at the Women's Sports Foundation for their generous help and for letting me enjoy the foundation's library while researching this book.

I also thank the people at the headquarters and public relations offices of the National High School Rodeo Association, the Women's Professional Rodeo Association, the Indianapolis Motor Speedway, *Chronicle* magazine, and Churchill Downs for their kind help with resources and answers to my questions.

My deepest gratitude to the people who allowed me to interview and quote them in this book.

J.E.G.

SPORTS HEROES AND FAIR PLAY

1

Who are your favorite sports heroes? This question was asked in a poll conducted by *Sports Illustrated for Kids*. More than eight thousand readers responded to the poll, and for the second year in a row, Shaquille O'Neal of the Orlando Magic was voted the favorite of all the athletes that kids admire. That's not terribly surprising, and he certainly deserves credit for being a good role model; what may be surprising, however, is that both girls and boys responded to this poll.

The young teens who took the time to respond to the poll provided the following interesting statistics. For boys, the top three athletes named were Michael Jordan, Shaquille O'Neal, and Shawn Kemp; they also admired Ken Griffey, Jr., Emmitt Smith, Frank Thomas, and Troy Aikman. For girls, the top three athletes named were Shaquille O'Neal, Michael Jordan, and Shawn Kemp. Yes, you read that correctly, not one woman made the top three list for girls or for boys! How could that be? Surely some women athletes are admired and considered role models? Why don't we see names like Nancy Kerrigan, FloJo, Jackie Joyner-Kersee, Kristi Yamaguchi? Two female names did at least make the top five of the girls' list—Nancy Kerrigan (figure skating) and Shannon Miller (gymnastics).

The same survey shows that the sport most young teens like to watch and play is basketball. Both girls and boys agree on the popularity of basketball, but girls also said they like to play soccer, baseball, and softball, while boys chose baseball, football, and soccer to complete their lists.[1] The coaches of the

***B**asketball is often named as the most popular sport for young people. Here, a girls' after-school-league team practices.*

Women's "Dream Team," as the USA Women's National Basketball Team is being called, will be happy to see how many girls want to play basketball.

Eleven women were chosen from the twenty-four who tried out in May of 1995 for this one-time basketball program designed to develop a talent pool prior to the 1996 Olympic selections. The dream team included two former Olympians, Teresa Edwards and Katrina McClain, and had many former college greats, such as Rebecca Lobo of the NCAA Championship University of Connecticut basketball team. These women were coached by Tara Van Derveer, the head coach at Stanford University. Maybe the next *Sports Illustrated* survey will include some of these women, and perhaps the successful Women's Olympic Gold "Dream Team" will be listed among teen favorites.

WOMEN IN SPORTS

The need to help both girls and boys see women as athletes is one reason for this book. Another reason is to make readers aware of the long and rich history of women as athletes, especially in North America. Historians cannot determine the exact date that the first sport or sports were played; however, if sports are broadly defined as physical exertion for the purpose of recreation and not work, then we know sports have been played since ancient times. The history of sports dates back at least to the original Greek Olympics in 776 B.C. Although women were not allowed to participate in those games, young girls and unmarried women could compete in games to honor Hera, goddess of women and the Earth.

It would take more than this book to detail all the information on women in sports that is available in public libraries and through sports foundations and universities. If we define sports as any physical recreational activities, fishing, hiking, and hunting would have to be included, in addition to organized sports with rules, sophisticated equipment, and timing and scoring devices. Because it would be impossible to fit everything between the covers of this book, some limits have been set. This book offers a chronological survey of women who participate as players, coaches, or leaders in the organization of sports or in the efforts for equality in sports and in American history. It begins with sports played by Native American women and ends with a look at careers in sports fields for today's female high school athletes and students, and also provides information about college scholarships. Readers will also learn about women who broke barriers in many sports, the triumphs and tragedies of sports, and how the athletic experience of many women has helped them develop athletic skills, a winning spirit, and the power to compete in all fields of life.

Women who broke barriers of gender and color through their efforts and accomplishments are good examples of women helping themselves and others through their determination and skills. Biographical information, sports statistics, and the contributions of individual women, groups, and sports associations also form integral parts of this book.

SPORTS AND LIFE

The skills athletes learn are not used just on the courts and playing fields; these skills help athletes to compete and win throughout life. For example, have you ever felt that math class is impossible and no one can help you understand algebra? Many athletes use a technique called visualization before a game or event. They picture themselves going through a perfect routine or game. They "see" themselves in moves and plays so they will be better able to execute the plays during the game. This same technique can work in math if you tell yourself you can solve the problem (never say "I can't do that!"). Ask yourself, how can I do the next part of the problem, how can I "see" this problem or a word problem so I can complete it? Visualizing helps make the confusing or difficult clearer and helps you solve the problem by thinking your way through it, just as athletes try to do before a game. Developing strategies for teamwork and individual performances can also help girls develop skills for future careers. Many female chief executive officers of Fortune 500 companies and businesses identified themselves as "tomboys" when they were

Sports participation yields many benefits—including the fun and excitement of playing (and sometimes winning) the game. Here, the winners line up for photographs after a college swim meet.

young girls and said that being athletes has helped them in their business careers.[2]

In the last several years, the world of sports has taken on aspects of big business, with athletes getting huge payments to endorse all kinds of products, from headache pills to milk to sneakers, soup, and golf clubs. Any magazine reader or television viewer can attest to the boom in ads by companies such as Nike, Reebok, Danskin, and even Campbell's soup. But using women sports stars to endorse products and creating advertising that appeals to women is fairly new in the advertising business. Major advertisers, however, have now caught on to the fact that women are not just playing golf and doing aerobics. The medical and educational professions are now taking a closer look at sports and exercise for women, and some interesting facts have emerged. Girls who participate in sports develop higher levels of self-esteem and are more likely to score well on achievement tests. Athletic girls are also more likely to stay in school and go on to attend college.

TITLE IX PROTECTIONS AND PROMISES

The opportunities you have to participate in high school sports are available in large part due to a federal law, Title IX of the 1972 Education Act. Before enactment of Title IX, high schools and colleges consistently and stubbornly maintained that males playing football or basketball could be treated better than female athletes because those two sports made money for the school. All schools in the United States are now required to offer equal opportunities for girls in sports programs.

What can you do if you think your school is unfair about athletic opportunities or coverage of these events? It is important to remember that all schools have watched their athletic programs dwindle due to cuts in educational budgets. If, however, girls' teams are paying for their own uniforms, the boys' teams better be as well! Talk to the athletic director or school principal about your concerns. If this initial step doesn't bring results, try the board of education, reminding each member of the board of Title IX requirements. Letters to local newspapers stating the problem and your goals might be helpful as well.

Another way to participate in sports is by coaching younger girls' teams. Many high schools now require students to serve a number of volunteer hours to graduate, and working with a young team is a great way to meet your hours. You can be a friend to a young girl who is trying to balance a rigorous, time-consuming sport with school responsibilities. Talking to her about how you achieved this balance may be helpful, but you might also drive her to practice or to a tutor and attend games to cheer her on. Many young girls are joining teams, and the choices of activities have increased tremendously. More women are going to colleges and universities on athletic scholarships than ever before. This gradual change was spurred by your mothers (and fathers) and grandmothers (and grandfathers) who wanted to play sports themselves but had fewer opportunities to do so. They recognized the values sports offer and have supported girls' efforts to participate.

More work still needs to be done. Men still receive two-thirds of the scholarship money awarded in athletics, and the sports budgets at most schools are still lower for women than for men. Most colleges allot only one-fourth of the total sports budget to women's sports, and recruiting budgets are much lower for women's sports than for men's. Fewer than 50 percent of the coaches for women's college sports are women, and fewer than 21 percent of college athletic directors are women. Local television stations still allot over 90 percent of their sports coverage to men's sporting events, and fewer than 1 percent of coaches for men's college sports are women.[3] These facts confirm the need to continue to press for equal opportunities.

These inequities might disappear if women continue to make themselves seen and heard in tennis, skating, rodeos, horse racing, skiing, swimming, golf, track and field, basketball, volleyball, soccer, archery, and every other sport. Media coverage of the Olympics and Paralympics, as well as marathons, skating competitions, and other sporting events,

THE EARLY YEARS 2

*C*olonial American women did participate in sports occasionally; although these women were limited by their amount of leisure time and by the standards of the day. Most men of the time believed that because women were the "weaker sex," a daughter or wife could not do all her work and still have energy for vigorous physical exercise. Some women, however, did find the time and the energy, as shown in records of women taking part in the horse races and hunts which were popular sports of the late 1700s.

If we look at life during the period of this country's development, we see that women were involved in a variety of sports as part of the cultures in which they lived. For example, since wealthier women in the South had servants and slaves to do most of the housework, the plantation wife was able to take walks, participate in dances, ride horses, and be a spectator at horse races. Dancing was a very important skill for women in the southern colonies, and fathers even went so far as to leave instructions in their wills that their daughters receive dancing lessons. Wealthy women danced the pavan and minuet. Dances for the less wealthy were not as structured as those of the rich. Middle-class southerners had a good time dancing jigs and reels, while the lower classes danced to "Turkey in the Straw" and the "Virginia Reel." Some southern women, especially in the Chesapeake area of Maryland, even took part in horse races, competing for special "ladies" prizes.

Most sports historians agree that sports as we know them

today were only beginning to develop in the colonial period and were not really part of everyday life. Horse races were probably the only organized sports activity for women that was considered acceptable in northern, middle, and southern colonies. A race was a big event and one that women looked forward to with much anticipation. They generally did not bet on the races, but being there afforded women many opportunities to be seen in their latest fashions and to experience the thrill of the race. Women and men were often seated separately, while African-Americans were relegated to seats on the fences at races that drew big crowds.[1]

Creating America's early settlements was an all-consuming effort. All able members of a family worked to build the home and start the farm or business. Regardless of why the settlers came, they brought with them the customs and traditions of their earlier home country. If you were a Puritan in England, then you were a Puritan in America and your status as a woman was very low. Women were treated virtually the same in America as they had been in Europe; for the most part, they worked in the home and had little opportunity for recreation.

If you were a woman living in the New Netherlands, you were lucky to be able to skate occasionally on the frozen lakes and rivers and perhaps even be in a skating race. Few other colonies accepted skating as an appropriate activity for women. Most colonials felt that swimming also was unacceptable for women. With bathing suits unknown at the time, swimming or "bathing" in a river or bay would be quite difficult in the clothing worn by colonial women. Where swimming was permitted, women and men were kept apart and women didn't swim but merely waded in the water. The recreational activities in which women did engage were not given much attention. A woman's role was to be a wife and mother, so what women did with their very limited leisure time was not usually recorded by the men who kept the records of that time. But records or no records, we do have diaries and letters from women of the colonial period, and we do know it is human nature to be playful. For this time period, the definition of sports needs to be very liberal, and should include any type of recreational activity for women.

For wealthier women, life was centered around the family, as was recreation. Charades, card games, and playing musical instruments were common leisure pursuits. Women even gambled on their card games! Holidays and weddings provided occasions for many people to gather in groups to go off sailing, sleighing, or riding. Of course, dancing was a favorite recreation at such events.

Women of the middle classes could not afford such elegant parties, but their recreation time was often spent in group activities with family and friends, such as barn raisings. When harvesting was completed, parties began and dancing was included. Even Puritan women danced, although ministers objected to mixed dancing for fear it might lead to adultery. The horse races and dances that colonial women participated in were usually unorganized, although some newspapers did advertise ladies' races at country fairs. Certainly no woman of the time thought of participating in organized sports.

The traditional views of women and attitudes about their activities reflect the society in which white women lived. While most written records from the colonial period describe the world of elite white women, we do have some information about the leisure time and sports activities of both African-American women and Native American women.

African-American women living in slavery participated in sports when they were allowed the time. Mainly on Sundays or in the evenings, African-American women could take part in foot races, games, and dancing. Sometimes white farmers and planters arranged fairs at which African-American women competed in races to win prizes—often including clothing. Holidays were a chance to relax and leave work behind for a day, and offered occasions for dancing and playing games.

Shinny and double ball were two field ball games played by Native American women. In both games, women formed two opposing teams, and the winning team was the one that scored the most goals by using a stick to get a ball or balls through the opponent's goal.

Shinny, which was played in nearly every Native American culture on the continent, is like field or ice hockey. A small buckskin or wooden ball, or a flattened disk, was dropped on the ground by an umpire, often the medicine man, and then the teams would try to hit or kick the disk through the opponent's goal to score. Four goals won the game. Teams consisted of ten to fifty players, who used long-handled wooden sticks curved at the bottom. Double ball was a faster and more difficult variation of this game and resembled lacrosse, which Native American men played and which is now popular nationwide. Two balls or disks were tied together and had to be scooped up and thrown with a stick. Shinny is still played by Native American girls today, and some Indian boarding schools have teams that compete with each other.

The women also played football and soccer-like games, using their feet to move the ball. Other popular ball games included juggling and tossing a ball with baskets. Often a few women would play at keeping a small, 3 to 5-inch (7.6 to 12.7-cm) ball in the air by hitting it with their hands.

The ball in these games sometimes symbolized the Earth, the Sun, or the Moon, and carried religious significance. When the game was of ceremonial importance, women usually did not participate as players, but they were permitted as spectators and sometimes wagered on the outcome.

Men and women usually played separate games, but occasionally they played on the same team in a game that resembled modern basketball. Handball and football games were played in all seasons, on the ground or on ice-covered waterways. Running games and ball games were major recreational activities in Native American cultures. The ceremonial aspects of most of the

*A*long with a variety of ball games, canoe races were a popular sport for some Native American women.

Native American games have been diluted or lost over the years, but the recreational aspects remain.[2]

NEW HORIZONS

By the late 1770s, a few American women, including Abigail Adams, were beginning to feel the restraints of their time and to wish for more opportunities to gain an education—and to get out of the kitchen. By the turn of the century, women were able to attend educational institutions outside of the home, but for the most part they learned only sewing, music, and other arts.

Little changed until 1833, when Oberlin College admitted its first women students; four years later, as Oberlin's first women graduated, Mount Holyoke Seminary in Massachusetts admitted women. Both schools offered a real academic curriculum, and at Mount Holyoke this included calisthenics and gymnastics. Outdoor exercise was also encouraged.

Great changes began appearing in the 1840s with the movement for women's rights, led by Elizabeth Cady Stanton, Susan B. Anthony, and Lucretia Mott. In their publications and speeches in support of women's rights, these women and their followers wrote and spoke about women and their physical considerations. They believed women had a right to both high mental and physical development. However, anyone looking at a picture of the clothing worn in this time period would wonder how a woman could exercise in all the layers she was expected to wear. This was a complaint among women from the early 1800s until the invention of bloomers.

Amelia Jenks Bloomer, editor of the journal *The Lily,* advocated dress reform and began writing about a costume for women that consisted of full pantaloons worn beneath a short skirt. The outfit made all forms of exercise possible and was also a statement about women's rights by those women brave enough to stand up to society and wear it. It was also about this time that women began trying to find ways into the traditionally male professions. Dr. Elizabeth Blackwell was the first woman to graduate from a U.S. medical school. She too wrote that better health comes from exercise and that schools should adopt active sports for boys and girls.[3]

With young women for the first time confined to school desks for long periods each day, the need for proper exercise became a growing concern. Between 1820 and 1860 many health reformers took up the issue. Catharine Beecher was one of the first and most influential. She lectured on the exercise needs of females and founded the Hartford Female Seminary in Connecticut in 1824. Her system of calisthenics was practiced at the seminary, and her book, *Physiology and Calisthenics for Schools and Families,* published in 1856, became famous and was used by many other schools.

By the start of the Civil War, women were moving into more of the historically male professions, such as teaching and nursing. They were also exercising more but were often criticized as "unwomanly," or told that working one part of the body would drain the blood from the rest of the body and thus be damaging. Intellectual exercise was attacked too, and it was even said that thinking too hard could cause all the blood to rush to a woman's head, making her unable to take care of her home and family! Many medical men agreed and feared that education for women would create monsters with large brains and tiny, weak bodies. They also feared that so much thinking would cause physical ailments and digestive problems. Women's rights advocates were appalled and spoke out against these views.

Fortunately, not everyone accepted these ideas of the dangers of exercise for women, and changes continued to develop in college athletics and sports activities for women. Matthew Vassar, founder of Vassar Female College, recognized that calisthenics was not sufficient physical activity for women. Vassar provided opportunities for riding and games, and by 1862 women were participating in sports competitions. Women at Vassar could also participate in bowling, boating, and swimming, although required to wear "modest" clothing. Soon other women's schools, including Wellesley (1870), Smith (1875), and Bryn Mawr (1885), followed Vassar's lead and encouraged sports for women to promote good health as part of good scholarship.

The last four decades of the nineteenth century brought sweeping changes to the women's sports scene. The lawn game of croquet became a popular and fashionable recreation for women. Although croquet is not a vigorous sport, it does require some skill to play it well. This game was developed in France by a doctor who wanted his patients, who were mostly invalids, to have some outdoor recreation. Croquet was one of the first recreational sports introduced in the United States after the Civil War. As a game that both men and women could play, croquet caught on quickly, and croquet wickets appeared on lawns everywhere. It was a social activity and a game, and it offered a chance to meet members of the opposite sex. Oberlin College offered coed classes in the sport, but its popularity lasted only about twenty years.

Women began to try a range of new sports, including rowing and pedestrianism, a precursor to modern racewalking. Two sixteen-year-old girls in Pittsburgh drew a large crowd in 1870 at their racewalking contest. The winner, Littie McAlice, claimed a gold watch and chain and two thousand dollars as the prize. In 1876, Mary Marshall from Chicago became a professional pedestrian, a sport that required endurance but not speed. She participated in many matches against women for rather large sums of money, as much as one thousand dollars per match. When Peter L. Van Ness, also a pedestrian, was in New York at the same time as Mary, she challenged him to a three-day race for a five-hundred-dollar prize. He accepted, and on November 16, 1876, they raced. Peter quickly took the lead but didn't hold onto it for long. After three days of individual races, Mary had won. By 1885 roller skating was also a favorite pastime for working girls and college girls.[5]

In the colleges, especially at Wellesley, three main types of exercise systems were used.

> Swedish gymnastics—based on a therapeutic model like that of Sweden. These were aerobic and stretching exercises and synchronized exercises.
>
> German gymnastics—military style routines using heavy equipment such as weighted balls.
>
> Sargent exercises—a program of strength-developing exercises designed by Dudley Allen Sargent, the director of the Hemenway Gymnasium at Harvard.

The Sargent system was most popular in the 1880s, but by

Gymnastics—as practiced in the gymnasium at the Woman's Medical College of Pennsylvania

the 1890s the Swedish style was more widely used and colleges began building gymnastics facilities.

The increasing interest in women's sports, and the availability of the facilities, paved the way for a number of important new sports. Two of these new sports were tennis and golf, which suddenly became popular sports for women as well as for men. The national women's amateur golf tournament was started in 1885, and the national women's outdoor tennis tournament was established in 1887. Within twenty-five years there were three hundred clubs in the Lawn Tennis Association, and national champions included Charlotte "Lottie" Dod and Dorothea Lambert. Archery and tennis were adopted by women's schools and were also played by women in coeducational colleges. Archery was considered an appropriate sport because it was not too strenuous and because women could practice alone or with men. The lack of physical contact made it acceptable for both single and married women. Clubs and a number of colleges, including Goucher, held matches and awarded medals. Colleges formed all sorts of sports teams and clubs; the University of California even had a women's football (soccer) club in 1877.

In the West, women actually competed with men in shooting contests. Phoebe Anne Oakley Moses, or as most of us know her, Annie Oakley, was one of the most skilled women shooters; she could outshoot many men. At age fifteen she won a target-shooting match against a marksman named Frank Butler. A year later they married and started the touring company of Butler and Oakley. By 1885, Oakley and her husband, now her manager, joined Buffalo Bill Cody's Wild West Show. Oakley was an excellent horsewoman who rode and acted in *The Western Girl*—a stage melodrama performed with an Indian pony—for the Wild West Show. One of her admirers was Chief Sitting Bull who made her his adopted daughter and named her "Little Straight Shooter." On the western frontier, women were often more daring in their sports, including riding, mountain climbing, and taking long hikes. Women also liked jackrabbit hunts, which were similar to the East Coast fox hunts, which were in turn modeled on those popular in England.

The East Coast had women sharpshooters, too. Rose Coghlan was a clay-pigeon shooter with an excellent shooting record.

She had been a target shooter but in 1887 decided to try trap shooting. The trap released a clay pigeon, and Rose would shoot it and several more as astonished men looked on.[5]

New and more sedate—but none-the-less competitive—games became available and drew larger numbers of women into sports. Golf had become popular in England and the United States and was usually played at membership clubs by the more affluent members of society. Women were restricted to the least popular times for their games and often had to keep to less attractive areas of the golf course. They had their own section of the clubhouse and often developed social networks of friends through golf.

Another sport was actually criticized by some as possibly leading young girls into prostitution! Regardless of this fear, bicycling soon became a popular sport and provided women with a new sense of physical freedom. The bicycle gave women a method of transportation that could take them places they could not have reached by walking. Women, therefore, began to look at the bicycle as a method of gaining mobility. The bicycle craze coincided with women making greater strides in entering professions and with a general increase in sports activities.

Since it was almost impossible to ride a bicycle in the typical female clothing of the day, many women riders began to change the style of dress by leaving off their corsets and wearing fewer underskirts. To the dismay of many men and women, some female bike riders wore scandalous knickers (knee-length pants) or bloomers.

The first bicycle, a form of wooden scooter, was called a *célérifère* and was invented in 1790 in France. By 1816, Baron Karl von Drais of Germany had invented an improved bicycle called a *draisienne*. This model had a steering bar connected to the front wheel. An improvement was made by a Scottish blacksmith, Kirkpatrick Macmillan, when he added foot pedals in 1839. The next model appeared in 1870 and was a high-wheeler, with a front wheel as big as 5 feet (1.5 m) across and a small back wheel. The safety bicycle was first commercially produced in England in

1885 by J. K. Starley. It had two wheels of the same size and was thus safer than earlier models. Pedals drove the rear wheel by means of a chain and sprockets, and the bike looked very much like those of today. By 1890, air-filled rubber tires and other improvements, like coaster brakes and adjustable handlebars, had about four million American women and men riding bicycles.

As less-constraining forms of dress made exercise more accessible, women found more sports to enjoy. Walking, hiking, climbing, ice skating, and fishing became popular exercises for women. Swimming was suddenly considered an excellent sport, as long as the bathing suit covered as much as possible. Bathing in cold water was thought to help blood circulation, and some even thought it promoted fertility in women.

Women who were active in feminist groups now looked to sports as a way to further their chances of gaining suffrage rights. They spread the word that organized sports and all forms of recreation or exercise were good for a woman's health. It was thought that these activities would even increase a woman's ability to be a strong wife and mother, and allow young women to work off sexual urges.

These inventions and new sports helped open a new era for women at the end of the nineteenth century. Images of Victorian women swathed in clothing and unable to move more than a few feet without overexerting themselves were disappearing. College athletics encouraged women to be active and proved to the disbelievers that women could develop mind and body and be better for it. As athletic facilities were expanded and women became more outspoken, their interest in sports grew along with their interest in their rights. Both of these female movements would continue to grow side by side and benefit from each other. Although women were still not competing in sports on the same level as men and female athletes were still a minority among women, more female sports, competitions, and freedoms were to come as the twentieth century approached.

NEW GAMES FOR THE NEW WOMAN

3

*T*he 1880s and 1890s ushered in new games and new enthusiasm for some of the older games. Women in the West and the East were active in sports, and colleges moved from offering calisthenics and a few team sports to developing organized competitive programs for women. At the University of California, a Young Ladies Lawn Tennis Club was organized, and a woman, Genvra Magee, was hired as an assistant in physical culture. Another woman, Phoebe Hearst, donated funds to build a gymnasium in which Magee could hold classes. Now women had a facility and a teacher.[1]

BASKETBALL BEGINS

Tennis wasn't the only popular sport. A new game was invented that used a soccer ball and two boxes, one placed at each end of a gym court. This was the start of basketball, created by James A. Naismith, who in 1891 was a physical education teacher at the School for Christian Workers in Springfield, Massachusetts. Naismith was asked to invent a game that could be played indoors during the winter months. His game was a bit clumsy at first, as suitable boxes couldn't be found and peach baskets were used instead. The baskets were attached to a balcony railing ten feet above the gym floor. He made up thirteen rules for the game, and his classes began playing. Dr. Naismith then introduced the game to the women of Vassar, and it quickly became a primary sport at the college. Within two years basketball had caught on at the other schools, and with some changes to improve the equipment and playing techniques, the game became more like the one we know today.

The game as the men originally played it was quite violent and intense, but Alice Foster spoke to the American Physical Education Review in 1897 and insisted that women could play basketball properly and thus avoid physical strain. The game was altered to make it safer for women. The playing floor was divided into three parts and players stayed in their own section rather than running the whole court. Players could dribble only three times and could hold the ball for only three seconds. Also, grabbing the ball from another player's hands was forbidden, as was touching another player. These rules remained as the standard of play, although some modifications were developed after the formation of the National Official Women's Basketball Committee.

Women's basketball caught on so quickly that basketball came to be considered a game only for girls, and sometimes boys refused to play it. Each of the women's college teams played slightly different versions of the game, and this prevented Bryn Mawr, Radcliffe, Vassar, and Lake Forest from having interschool competitions.

Few news articles can be found about the early women's basketball games because they were little known outside of the colleges prior to 1900. However, the sport was played at schools on both coasts, with teams of up to ten women. Basketball was enormously popular with the women students and was a change from less intense and less competitive athletics. It allowed women to develop physical stamina and also taught them teamwork. At the Western colleges, which were coeducational, basketball was seen as a way for women to compete in sports. The Eastern colleges would not allow intercollegiate competition because they feared for the health and welfare of the women. This fear contributed to keeping women out of the Olympics until the early 1900s, and even then basketball was not included.

*T*he basketball team of the Smith College class of 1899 playing the team of the class of 1902 before an enthusiastic crowd of female spectators.

Under the leadership of Senda Berenson, interclass games of basketball took place at Smith College. Berenson, who was born in Lithuania, came to America with her family in 1875. She attended the Boston Normal School of Gymnastics and then found a teaching job at Smith. Berenson is credited with developing the general rules for women's basketball.

While at Smith, Berenson had the first- and second-year students play each other in March of 1893. The first-year students won. By the late 1890s, these interclass competitions filled the college gymnasiums with spectators, each team's colors were displayed, and over a thousand fans came to watch girls play basketball.

On April 4, 1896, women students at the University of California and at Stanford University played against each other in the first officially recorded women's varsity basketball game. The outcome of this game, played at the Armory Hall in San Francisco, was Stanford 2–1 over the University of California. Male spectators were not allowed to watch the game.[2]

Basketball was helping to shape a new attitude toward women and sports. Physical education teachers began to view athletics for women in a different light, emphasizing active teamwork more and calisthenics less.

Overcoming poor facilities, lack of finances, different rules, outright discouragement, and fear for the moral character of young girls, basketball was soon being played in high schools also. Basketball, like many other high school girls' sports, started as an after-school club activity that was usually run by the girls themselves. Once varsity teams began developing in the high schools, the coaches were almost always men. Eventually, more women were trained in physical education and took over many of the coaching duties. Baseball, which started shortly before basketball, actually took a dip in popularity as basketball became the most popular sport for women.[3] Basketball, however, wasn't the only competitive sport, and baseball was played along with track and field. New sports teams developed as women became more interested in sports and the freedom to participate grew.

THE BASEBALL GAME

A group of girls from Vassar, once again, were not content to watch men playing the game of baseball but wanted to play themselves. Thus women's baseball began.[4] A few baseball clubs existed as early as 1870, and in the 1880s Harry H. Freeman tried, but failed, to launch a team of women baseball players. Too many people feared Mr. Freeman's motives, some even thinking the girls were being recruited as prostitutes. As baseball progressed at Vassar it also caught on at Smith College, where a student, Minnie Stephens, had to steal a bat from a group of boys in order to play. By 1892, the Smith women were playing baseball and had their own equipment.

HOCKEY ON THE FIELD

Another sport that became popular at the turn of the century had its start at expensive private schools in the Northeast, but it didn't take long for field hockey to be adopted by girls of all economic classes. One woman, Constance M. K. Applebee, deserves the credit for making field hockey a wide-spread sport. Sometimes called Connie or "the Apple," she introduced field hockey to private colleges in the northeastern part of the United States. She held the first demonstration of the game in a courtyard next to the Harvard University gymnasium. Applebee also founded field hockey's national organization, the United States Field Hockey Association.

In the summer months, Applebee ran a camp for hockey players in the Pocono Mountains of Pennsylvania. During the winter she taught at Bryn Mawr College and also traveled to other colleges, introducing and coaching the game. The sport was considered nonviolent and healthful, but the clothes were a problem. Applebee told her players to leave off their petticoats and wear skirts six inches above the ground. The sport became so popular that by 1901, Bryn Mawr, Wellesley, Radcliffe, and Vassar all had field hockey clubs.

INTO THE WATER

As women continued looking for sports and athletic activities, they often returned to older sports and modernized them. Swimming was a sport women had enjoyed, in a modest way, since colonial days. Women, then, had waded or bathed in rivers and lakes, often holding onto a rope as they bobbed up and down. Now the water was seen as another sports arena, and women were encouraged to learn the basics of swimming. As well as enjoying the sport, skilled swimmers could handle themselves in deep water and rescue nonswimmers in trouble.

Swimming had few rules and could be learned without an instructor, two aspects that made the sport inviting. Books and magazine articles instructed women that it was safe to wade out into the water until it was chest high. Instructions for back swimming, treading water, and floating were included in a book in which Harriet Ayers informed readers that swimming was healthy for women. Many women became good swimmers, but the sport remained a recreational one as facilities were poor and few schools offered formal instruction. Some colleges had lakes on campus that women could use, but it remained an informal activity until the late 1800s. In 1886, lessons were given at the Brooklyn Normal School, and by 1890, a swim club was started at Westchester College in New York State.

Although women's swimming did not become a popular spectator sport until the 1920s, women by then had been establishing swimming records for fifty years! Most of these were long-distance records, and many were achieved in England. In New York, in August of 1887, six girls competed in a 1-mile (1.6 km) swim along Coney Island Beach. The *New York Times* reported on the contest and noted that the girls ranged in age from eleven to sixteen and that cash prizes from five to twenty dollars were awarded.[5] Women's swimming took on a new status when women were called upon to replace male lifeguards at beaches when the men went to serve in World War I.

One swimmer who shocked many society women of the turn of the century was Eleanora Sears. Sears was an excellent athlete and enjoyed giving society a bit of a tweak with a 4.5-mile

(7.2-km) swim from Bailey's Beach to First Beach along the Newport, Rhode Island, shore. A great-great-granddaughter of Thomas Jefferson, she played golf and polo, tennis, skated, and sailed. She always chose to wear comfortable, if somewhat shocking, clothes for sports and didn't knuckle under when other women said she dressed in unladylike clothes. Eleanora Sears was such a good tennis player that she won the national doubles four times, the mixed doubles once, and was a finalist in other contests.

THE TENNIS GAME

The game of "balls and rackets" came to America in the spring of 1874, brought here by Miss Mary Outerbridge. While visiting a British military installation in Bermuda, Mary played a game of balls and rackets with some of the soldiers. This game was a modification of the tennis played at garden parties in England, and Mary liked it immediately. Before leaving Bermuda in 1874, she bought a net, racket, and balls to take back to New York. Fortunately, her brother was a director of the Staten Island Cricket and Baseball Club, and she was able to use a corner of the club grounds to lay out a tennis court. Tennis was quickly accepted by women for the traditional reasons—it was not too competitive, it could be played at a slow and dignified pace, the clothing was appropriate to the times, and a lady could glide after the ball without seeming to run.

Tennis quickly caught on at the female colleges, and courts were built for women to play on. Clubs developed and women crowded the courts to play. Smith College held its first Tennis Tournament in October of 1882. They even charged admission— two hairpins (used to pin down the tape that outlined the court).[6]

Since the equipment was not too costly, tennis could be played by women from a range of economic classes. By 1894, many towns had tennis clubs, and most women were eager to

*A*n early star of women's tennis, Eleanora Sears was also a
noted swimmer.

play the sport. Some women enjoyed the sport for the purely
social aspects and really never developed their athletic abilities;
others developed a high level of skill. Championship tournaments were held, and the United States Lawn Tennis Association
(USLTA) was formed.

One of the first tennis greats was a young woman who had been in poor health as a girl. Her doctor recommended that she get outside and play to build up her strength. Hazel Hotchkiss lived on a remote ranch in Healdsburg, California, with only her four brothers for playmates. By the time her family moved to Berkeley, she had developed into a strong player of most sports. Her parents thought the ladylike game of tennis would be good for her and encouraged her to practice in front of their garage. In just six months, Hazel was entering women's tournaments and winning. She developed new tactics for the game, including moving around the court more, and even beat the reigning stars of California tennis, the Sutton sisters.

After marrying, Hazel Hotchkiss Wightman established the Wightman Cup in 1923, for women's competition worldwide. She won scores of championships, including the national senior doubles title in 1954 and continued playing tennis into her eighties. At age eighty-seven, she received an award from the queen mother of England. She was elected to the International Tennis Hall of Fame in 1957.

ON THE GOLF COURSE

The sport of golf was gaining popularity at this time. The Morris Country Club in New Jersey was started by women, as were many golf clubs of the 1890s. Most clubs allowed women members to have full membership, although they often restricted them to weekday play so men could play on Saturdays. Many clubs put in nine-hole courses for the women, who were thought to be less strong and not necessarily able to complete a whole course of eighteen holes. But once again, women showed what they could do.

In 1896, the Morris Country Club held a championship competition for women, which twenty-five women, including Beatrice Hoyt, entered. Hoyt could drive the ball 120 to 160 yards (109.7 to 146.3 m) and could out-drive most of the men at her club. Hoyt won that championship and many others.

Colleges didn't take to golf as quickly as they had to some of the other sports of this time period; however, some did put in links and organize clubs for women's golf. Wellesley and Smith were two of the first to organize clubs for their female students.

In response to the surge in sports activity, shoe manufacturers began creating shoes for women to wear while playing golf, tennis, and baseball. Sports equipment and clothing became a growth industry, one that is still growing today.

AND OTHER GAMES

With clothing more comfortable and sports more acceptable by the turn of the century, several other sports gained momentum, including roller-skating, ice skating, mountaineering, and bowling. More and more of the sports at this time freed women from restrictive clothing and from male dominance and allowed them to gain a sense of themselves as competitors.

Roller-skating was more of a fad than most sports of the time. It originated in Holland in the eighteenth century and was introduced to Americans in 1863 by an Englishman, James Plimpton. This was another sport that was first adopted by the social elite but which quickly caught on with all groups because it was inexpensive and required no training. Skating rinks were built in many cities, but by the late 1880s the interest began to die out and skating became more of a recreation for children.

Ice skating became popular on the colder college campuses where the women could try out their ability on the frozen lakes and ponds. Many young women were afraid to try skating for fear of looking foolish if they fell; however, by the end of the 1800s, families were enjoying this sport throughout the North and East, where winter months could be long and boring. Women became very skilled at gliding along on their iron-blade

A *magazine illustration from the early 1880s, "A Belle on Rollers," shows the then-popular sport of roller-skating.*

skates, but ice skating didn't develop into a competitive sport for several more years.

Women who wanted to experience the great outdoors and enjoyed rugged sports often took to walking through the mountains. Physical education teachers in schools and colleges encouraged this sport because in addition to providing exercise, it afforded the opportunity to observe nature. With proper measures, such as stout shoes and adequate food supplies, walking excursions also granted women a sense of independence.

In another sport, Wellesley college was once again in the lead. Its director of physical training, Lucille Hill, was among the first to encourage physical exercise through the sport of bowling. This sport appealed to society women as a means of spending an evening in an athletic activity in clubs with bowling alleys. Middle-class women were warned to be careful where they played this sport: it was vigorous, and public bowling alleys were often located near smoke-filled gambling and drinking halls. But women were encouraged by the women's magazine writers of the day, who described the glow bowling brings to the cheek and the physical exertion of bowling. By 1907, bowling had become popular among women, and a league was formed in St. Louis, Missouri. The Women's National Bowling Association was founded in St. Louis in 1916 and was the forerunner of the Women's International Bowling Congress.

A few early organizers of women's bowling were later inducted into the Women's International Bowling Congress Hall of Fame. Emily Chapman organized leagues and instructed women for thirty years or more. Addie Ruschmeyer bowled for more than sixty years and was a charter member of the Greater New York City Women's Bowling Association. Deane Fritz and Grace Smith won many championships and helped to pioneer the game. Women made bowling one of their sports and continued on their quest to be recognized as athletes.

TRACK AND FIELD AND SWORDS

Other athletic activities and events were soon being taken up by college women. Vassar was in the lead for track and field competitions. As early as 1895, field days were held at Vassar and also at the University of Nebraska, where photographs show women in track and field events. Women participated in jumping hurdles, shot putting, and even pole vaulting.

Women's fencing began in the United States as a fad in New York, about 1894. Clubs including the Berkeley Athletic Club and the Fencers Club of New York offered fencing classes and private lessons. This was an expensive sport and appealed to wealthy society women, who may have been more interested in the fancy costumes and equipment than the sport itself. Regardless of their motivation, they did participate in the sport, and it became an Olympic event in 1904.

OPENING THE OLYMPIC GATES

The ancient Olympic Games were revived in 1896 by Baron Pierre de Coubertin, who established the modern games to encourage world peace and friendship and to promote amateur athletics—for men only. Coubertin called for the young amateur sportsmen of the world to come to Athens, Greece, for the first modern Olympics, but he excluded females as anything but spectators. Coubertin was a man of his times and held very Victorian views about women. He disapproved of women in sports and thought the only proper role for women was motherhood. He did not believe women should be involved in public competitions, and he fought against their participation in the Olympics for three decades, even after women were allowed to begin competing in the 1900 Olympic Games in Paris, France, which included women's golf and tennis. The 1900 Olympics were held as part of a World Exhibition in Paris, and the International Olympic Committee (IOC) and the Baron were overruled about women's participation. Margaret Abbott of the United States won a gold medal in golf—the first American woman to achieve this.

Slowly, women gained ground in the Olympics. In 1904, women's archery and fencing were added. In London, England, the 1908 Olympics included women's tennis, archery, and figure skating. Most of the women participants were British, and Lottie Dod won a silver medal in archery. Swimming was not yet included, which seems to have stemmed from a reluctance to have women so scantily dressed in public. The organization of the Federation Internationale de Natation Amateur (FINA) tried its best to get swimming into the Olympics, and finally, in 1912, in Stockholm, swimming was included.[7] Women competed in the 100-meter and the 400-meter races and also in platform diving. Due to World War I, the 1916 games, which been scheduled for Berlin, Germany, were cancelled. After the war, the games were held in Antwerp, Belgium, in 1920, and women were again allowed to participate in water sports and tennis. The Americans dominated the swimming and diving events but had disputes over the tennis rules and boycotted those matches. Constance Applebee formed a field hockey team in Philadelphia, Pennsylvania, and took its members to England. They lost eight of their ten matches, and their application for inclusion in the 1920 Olympics was rejected. Women's fencing was included in the 1924 Paris Summer Olympics, and by 1928 track and field and team gymnastics were allowed in the summer games in Amsterdam.

There were two main reasons for the changes in the status of women as athletes at the Olympics. First, Baron Coubertin retired as IOC president. Secondly, European women became determined to compete on the international level, and they hammered away at the IOC for inclusion.

Camille Blanc, the Mayor of Beauliu in Monaco, organized the first Olympiades Feminines in 1921. This was a separate (and unequal) competition for women. The main events for the contestants, who came from France, Italy, Switzerland, England, and Norway, were track and field and basketball. The games were held again the next year to the public's thorough enjoyment. Six hundred women from nine countries competed in 1922. The success of these games did not impress the IOC, and it wasn't until the early 1930s that women achieved greater inclusion and status in the Olympics.

ORGANIZING SPORTS

From the early days of amateur competitive sports until the late 1880s, there were some difficulties in determining exact rules for games, providing for proper judging, and defining amateur status. To correct these problems and others, the Amateur Athletic Union (AAU) was founded in 1888. It is now composed of district associations of clubs and schools, with a national headquarters in Indianapolis, Indiana. The AAU is the governing body for eight Olympic sports: track and field, aquatics, bobsled, boxing, judo, luge, weightlifting, and wrestling. The AAU conducts developmental programs for national and international competition in basketball, gymnastics, and many other sports.

Since 1930, the AAU has conducted an annual poll of sportswriters to choose the recipient of the Sullivan Award. Given in memory of one of the AAU's founders, James E. Sullivan, the award is presented to the amateur athlete who has done the most to advance good sportsmanship. Women have been some of the amateur athletes who have benefited from AAU leadership. Much of the development of sports and the growth of sports as an industry has occurred in the last seventy-five years. Organizations like the AAU helped make more concise sets of rules. These advances help women, but only because men are being helped first.

Women's athletics started in the colleges and moved to the sports clubs and finally to world competition, but it took nearly fifty years to achieve this. As women's educational opportunities expanded, they started looking for other fields to conquer. In sports, they learned the power of teamwork and the freedom gained through exercise. These changes brought about changes in society as a whole. The new woman of the late 1800s and early 1900s was living in the industrial age; immigration to the United States was bringing in new people and ideas and new time-saving inventions, and the growth of cities helped change the pace and style of life. The new culture of America provided time and desire for recreation, and women became healthier and freer. Once they got started in athletics, there was no stopping them.

SPORTS OF THE GOLDEN WOMEN

4

With women participating in the Olympics and America's prosperity growing after World War I, women athletes should have been headed for great heights. Many great women athletes did emerge as stars in the period between the two world wars, and the sports movement did indeed continue to grow; however, there were disagreements among the women who led the movement, and the priorities in women's sports seemed to have been off-track for a while.

In the United States, the governing body for amateur sports, the Amateur Athletic Union (AAU), supported and even encouraged women's participation in the Olympics. Although it hadn't always been in favor of women competing in the Olympics, in 1922 the AAU intended to send a team of female athletes to the Olympic Games. They were opposed by the physical education professionals who had been setting policy for female sports in the United States and who felt they should continue doing so. The Committee on Women's Athletics (CWA), which was part of the American Physical Education Association (APEA), opposed Olympic participation for two main reasons. First, the AAU was not a school-related organization, and schools had long been the center of women's sports. Secondly, in the Olympics, only a few, highly skilled women athletes could compete, which took opportunities away from average women who wanted to participate in athletic sports and events. The Women's Division of the National Amateur Athletic Federation (NAAF) was formed to promote a national policy that would regulate girls' and women's sports. A crucial part of their policy was to keep women out of the Olympics; they even petitioned the IOC to eliminate women's sports from the 1932 Olympics. They wanted women's sports kept in colleges, where they could maintain control. Although the petition was denied, the outlook for skilled athletes remained dim as physical educators continued to stress their opposition to removing sports from the control of the schools. While women had competed in several Olympics by this time, they had done so largely on their own and not as part of national teams.

Outstanding women athletes continued to develop in the years between the two world wars (1918–1939), but they often lacked good training fields, coaches, and equipment, since these were mostly tied to the universities. Women hoping for Olympic gold had to fund their own training and even organize their own competitions, which greatly limited the pool of women from which to develop Olympic talent.

Despite these handicaps, this period between the wars was an important era of widening horizons for women in varied areas. Female athletes did develop, and many "stars" or "golden women" caught the attention of Americans and the world. Several women made their marks in different athletic fields, creating a sports legacy for American women.[1]

THE GOLDEN WOMEN

AN ALL-AROUND SUPERSTAR

Most athletes, sportswriters, and fans would agree that the "golden woman" who stands out as the athlete and role model of the period was Mildred "Babe" Didrikson Zaharias. Mildred Didrikson is generally considered the greatest all-around woman athlete in history. Indeed, she wrote in her autobiography that her goal was to be the greatest athlete who ever lived.[2]

Born in Port Arthur, Texas, in 1914, she was the youngest of

Babe Didrikson, sailing over a hurdles course in a photograph from the early 1930s

seven children. Her parents and other siblings had immigrated to the United States from Norway. Her father worked as a furniture finisher; her mother spent much of her time trying to get her youngest daughter to wear dresses. But Didrikson was happier in overalls and continued trying every sport she could. During high school, she was on at least six teams, including swimming, tennis, golf, basketball, baseball, and volleyball. She did not finish high school but fortunately was able to continue sports on a team at Employers' Casualty Insurance Company, where she worked. The owner of the company, Melvorne Jackson McCombs, was a supporter of women's basketball. His company had a basketball team—the Golden Cyclones, whose members played in shorts and shirts—and he was married to one of the players. In 1930, McCombs hired Didrikson as a stenographer for a salary of $75 a month. She joined the Golden Cyclones and led the team to many victories, including the AAU championship within a year of joining the team. McCombs also sponsored a track team at her request, and by the time of the 1930 AAU national track championships, she was already known as a star athlete.

The 1932 Olympic Games, held in Los Angeles, California, were a triumph for Babe. The rules limited her participation to three events, and she did well in all of them. In the javelin competition she beat the world record by more than 2 meters (6.5 feet); she tied for first place in the high jump, and was given the gold medal for the 80-meter hurdles.

The press coverage at this time was very concerned with how the athletes looked, and articles often devoted more space and words to appearances than to skills. Babe was usually described as a tomboy, and the stories often referred to her boy's haircut and boyish body.

After the 1932 games, Babe was suspended from the AAU because her picture appeared in an advertisement for a car company. Babe explained that she hadn't known about the ad, but the AAU prevailed. In 1933 and 1934 she toured as a baseball player and had her own team, Babe Didrikson's All Americans. Also in 1934, she began to get serious about golf. This is the sport for which she is most remembered and which has contributed the most to her fame.

Largely due to Babe's skill and popularity, women's golf

attracted attention in the United States, and the Ladies' Professional Golf Association tour was organized. Didrikson married a wrestler, George Zaharias, but it was not a long marriage. She was diagnosed with cancer in 1953, but after an operation, she came back to win the National Women's Open and the Tam O'Shanter All-American tournaments in 1954. She died of cancer at the age of forty-two in 1956. She is remembered as one of the greatest athletes of the first half of the twentieth century—not just one of the greatest women athletes, but one of the greatest athletes.

A GOLDEN SKATER

Another "golden" woman and athlete of the years between the world wars was Sonja Henie. Although she is probably best remembered for her success in Hollywood as an ice-skating movie star in such films as *Sun Valley Serenade,* Sonja Henie was also an excellent athlete. She won Scandinavian championships in tennis and skiing and was adept at horseback riding, sprinting, and swimming. She amassed over a thousand cups, medals, and titles and won the figure-skating Olympic gold three times, in 1928, 1932, and 1936.

America's first figure-skating champion, Theresa Weld, won the national championship in 1914 and continued to participate in competitions as a skater or official through the 1920s. She was even nicknamed "Mrs. Figure Skater" after her marriage to Charles Blanchard. Perhaps her most important contribution to skating was her work as the editor of the magazine *Skating,* which appeared in 1923 and was widely read for fifty years.

A TENNIS STAR

Helen Wills Moody, born in 1905 in Berkeley, California, was a top female tennis player for nearly twenty years. Helen began playing tennis as a little girl because her best friend, a boy, loved

*A*n early star of the ice, Theresa Weld

the game. Her father supported her efforts, playing the game with her and getting beaten by the time she turned fourteen. Between 1923 and 1938 she won eight Wimbledon singles titles, seven U.S. singles titles, four French championships, and the gold medal at the Paris, France, 1924 Olympics. Her records would stand until 1990. As they commonly did with female athletes, the media bestowed a nickname, and Helen's was "Little Miss Poker Face," because she always appeared totally absorbed while on the tennis court. Helen preferred clothing such as sleeveless shirts and knee-length skirts, that allowed her freedom of movement on the courts. She weathered the storms of criticism that her clothing provoked, and she was able to appear on the court without the stockings and long skirts of the times. She was also a talented artist, illustrating her own autobiography, *Tennis,* and a superb academic student who cherished her Phi Beta Kappa key. She changed tennis play for women; her approach was to develop all strokes and play a more all-around game than had previously been the style. Helen Wills Moody's success at Wimbledon was not matched until 1990 with Martina Navratilova's ninth win.

SWIMMING THE CHANNEL

On August 6, 1926, the world had a new swimming record holder. Prior to that day, only six men had succeeded in swimming the English Channel, but now a 5-foot-5-inch (1.65 m) woman, Gertrude "Trudy" Ederle, became the first woman to swim the 20 miles (32.2 km) across the channel. She was nineteen years old, and she broke the previous records by completing her swim in only fourteen hours and thirty-one minutes! Two years earlier she had won a gold medal as part of the 1924 American 400-meter relay team. She was a strong athlete and the winner of many awards, and she flaunted her independence by rejecting the bathing attire of the early 1900s.

Gertrude Ederle swam the English Channel in record time—beating earlier male swimmers by about two hours.

Swimming was finally coming into its own as a sport, with the help of athletes like Trudy. No longer did women wear bloomers and Turkish dressing gowns as they delicately approached the water. They were competitors now and wore modest but less encumbering swim suits. The Women's Swimming Association of New York included many of the star swimmers of the 1920s, and American women took medals in the Olympics at Antwerp, Paris, and Amsterdam. Three of the best swimmers at this time were Helene Madison, Katherine Rawls, and Eleanor Holm.

Helene Madison won three gold medals at the Los Angeles Olympics, and during the 1930s she held twelve world and thirty American championships. At a height of 6 feet (1.83 m), this Seattle Washingtonian was known as the queen of the waters.

Katherine Rawls competed on both swimming and diving teams and eventually captured twenty-four swimming and five diving championships. A third member of the Olympic team in Los Angeles was Eleanor Holm, who won the gold medal in the backstroke. Eleanor is also remembered as an entertainer who was the swim star of the New York World's Fair Aquacade (a water show); she even played Jane in the Tarzan movies.

The James E. Sullivan Memorial Trophy for 1944 went to an eighteen-year-old, Ann Curtis, as the best amateur athlete of the year. Ann's career started when she was just an eleven-year-old swimmer in San Francisco competing in her first AAU girls' freestyle swimming championship. Her swimming career saw her win many championships and set many records, including becoming the first woman to swim 100 yards (91.4 m) in less than one minute. In the 1948 Olympics she won the 400-meter title and took two other medals. After retiring from amateur competition, she married and started her own swim club, teaching and coaching children to swim like champions.

ON THE SKI SLOPES

Leaving the pool and going to the ski slopes, our next golden sportswoman is Gretchen Fraser, a twenty-nine-year-old who gave America its first Olympic gold medal in skiing in 1948. Until Gretchen's rocket trip down the slopes of Mt. Piz-Nair in St. Moritz, Switzerland, Europeans had dominated skiing. This was Gretchen's first Olympic competition, and she was the first to ski the slalom event that day; taking on the untouched trail that could have been filled with hazards, such as hidden bumps or patches of ice. Her first run was slow, she had been too cautious; but the second run was 57.7 seconds and her combined time was less than two minutes. She had earned first place and a gold medal.

If your parents own a ski center, it's a pretty sure bet you will become a good skier. At the age of fifteen, Andrea Lawrence qualified for the 1948 U.S. Olympic slalom. She didn't win any medals but did meet the man she would marry three years later. At the 1952 Olympics, Andrea won two gold medals and barely missed a third. She became the only American skier to win two gold medals in a winter Olympics. Andrea was honored as an inductee of the International Women's Sports Hall of Fame.

WORKING TO PLAY

Although not all women athletes could make it to the Olympics or build record-breaking careers in the years between the world wars, changes in the way women viewed sports definitely occurred. Many hard-working and dedicated athletes existed in this country and throughout the world. But contemporary social attitudes declared that athleticism detracted from femininity. Sportswomen continued to fight this concept through the period. These attitudes, combined with the restrictions on how and where women were allowed to compete, led to the need for leagues and competitions that were not under the control of the Women's Division of the National Amateur Athletic Federation. Due to the strict rules for basketball created by the federation, which made it hard for all the women's teams to compete, and the attitude of most physical educators, women's collegiate sports were declining to the level of sports days rather than tournaments. Into this void stepped industrial sports.

Industrial employers became concerned with the health of their women workers and introduced physical activities to keep the workers healthy and thus keep the absentee rate down. Sports activities also helped create loyalty to the company; workers stayed in their jobs longer as team spirit from the field spilled over into the workplace. On the surface, it appears that these industry teams were a nice benefit for the workers, and they were; however, the original purpose, increasing productivity for the company, should be remembered.

The teams also provided public relations benefits for the companies. Fielding a team of women made a company seem benevolent as well as forward-looking about issues of health and equality. The teams were also great advertising since local favorite teams became identified with the company's product. This is similar to the way companies today proudly announce their sponsorship of America's Olympic athletes, thus creating a caring image in consumers' minds as well as fostering consumers' desires to be patriotic and buy the products.

Most industrial sports teams were led by men hired as activity and program directors. As more women were employed by companies, women began to fill the role of activities director; even then, however, these women were almost always under the supervision of a man. As the teams formed, team coaches and managers were men.

Industrial teams had been in existence as early as the first half of the 1800s, when women composed up to 80 percent of the labor force in northeastern cotton mills. Large numbers of female employees also worked in cigar factories and in the footwear industry. In the early 1800s, the cotton mills in Lowell, Massachusetts, housed many workers in company buildings, and other companies provided meeting rooms and libraries for recreation time.

By the late 1800s, large companies, such as Metropolitan Life Insurance Company of New York, had started teams for men. By the turn of the century, however, companies began to be concerned for the health of the women workers and introduced calisthenics and posture-improving classes. By 1894, the National Cash Register Company provided ten-minute calisthenics breaks for its female employees.

These practices eventually led to the industrial sports teams, and of these, bowling, softball, and basketball were the most popular. Different geographic regions of the country had their favorite sports, and loyalty to local teams ran very high.

INDUSTRIAL BOWLING

Bowling quickly became popular with men and women, partly due to the ease of learning the game and partly because only five people were needed for a team. Perhaps most importantly, women of any age could play, and a woman didn't need to be an outstanding athlete to get onto a bowling team. People in the large midwestern cities were especially fond of bowling, and alleys were often found in neighborhood bars. The Women's International Bowling Congress (WIBC) had a women's tournament in 1920 and offered $2,000 in prize money. Eighty-four teams entered the competition. Employers saw the bowling team as a morale booster and often scheduled competitions with other factory teams. Divisions were created for teams from factories, stores, and banks, and another for teams from churches and clubs. Ten thousand women bowlers from Chicago and neighboring towns entered the Chicago American Tourney in the 1930s. Bowling didn't receive much in the way of press coverage, possibly because the rosters of most teams were made up of factory workers instead of private athletic club members, and also because the players were women. Even if she didn't receive much press coverage for it, Jennie Kelleher of Madison, Wisconsin, bowled a perfect 300 game on February 12, 1930, and was credited with being the first woman to achieve this perfect score.[3]

As more women entered the workforce—following the invention of the typewriter and the start of World War II—companies added more sports to their programs, but bowling remained extremely popular. In 1943, nineteen hundred teams entered the WIBC tournament.

B*owling was a popular sport in many industries. Government workers also joined teams throughout the 1940s.*

Despite bowling's popularity, basketball was the most visible industrial sport, and its players got the largest share of public notice. Many Hall of Fame Basketball players began and ended their careers playing on industrial teams.[4] As the popularity of women's basketball spread in high schools and colleges, working women wanted to play the sport as well. Exactly when the women's industrial teams began is not certain; however, there were basketball teams playing by 1910. As with the other industrial sports, employers recognized that basketball teams would be good for their company's public relations, and commercially sponsored basketball teams became very popular. Because only a small number of women were attending college and working women rarely had sports clubs to join, the company team was an unusual opportunity for working women.

One of the most organized and competitive basketball groups was in the South. Textile mills of the southern region of the United States employed many women, and they also allowed the daughters of employees to play for their industrial teams. These female industrial basketball teams were given as much chance to play and develop skills and team spirit as the men's teams.

Each mill tried to sponsor at least one team, and the mills organized competitions against each other. This practice led to mills hiring women for their athletic skills, and some mills hired players away from the other mills' teams. Many employers even paid the women their wages while the team was on the road to play in competitions.

After World War I, the Southern Textile Basketball Tournament was founded and played its 1921 competition in Greenville, South Carolina. This tournament featured A (higher skill level) and B (average skill level) teams for men and an A team for women. Within ten years, this tournament had more than one hundred and fifty teams competing from five southern states, and a B team had been added for women. This Southern Textile Basketball Tournament played yearly (except for three years during World War II) and continued strongly into the 1970s, when college basketball became more dominant.

Industrial sponsorship of women's basketball helped lead to the founding of the Amateur Athletic Union (AAU) national basketball championship. However, some strange attitudes and practices were still apparent. For a time, the AAU championship included a beauty pageant in which the players were the contestants. Even in the 1930 AAU championships, the Basketball

Committee chairperson, Lyman Bingham, questioned the presence of women in sports and wondered how feminine they could be. Notes from the minutes of the committee's meeting include his remarks:

> *I too was skeptical and fully expected to see fainting girls carried away in ambulances . . . but I was agreeably pleased. What I actually did see was a group of girls at the end of the game rush to the center of the floor to cheer their opponents and then go arm and arm with them off the floor to appear later at a dance.*[5]

During the Depression, companies cut back on their sports teams, but few closed down their programs altogether. Even when colleges curtailed women's basketball, some women played on industrial teams, such as the ones sponsored by Coca-Cola and Yellow Cab in Memphis, Tennessee.

One of the best teams in the Southern Textile League was the Hanes Hosiery team. This was a great team in the 1940s and 1950s, with players including Eunies Futch and Evelyn Jordan. Both of these women were later on the United States women's basketball team at the 1955 Pan-American Games. Jordan and Futch also played softball for Hanes Hosiery.

INDUSTRIAL SOFTBALL AND BASEBALL

The official title of "softball" was first used in 1932, but women were playing the game long before that, and industrial softball teams were among the best. Some large industrial companies had their own softball leagues, with as many as eight teams composed of employees. Western Electric Company of Chicago, Illinois, had such a league in 1931. A union, the Amalgamated Clothing Workers, also in Chicago, sponsored women's teams as well. One team in Los Angeles, California, the Eaglettes, was an African-American women's team sponsored by the African-

American newspaper the *California Eagle.* Many other teams were sponsored by breweries (A.B.C. Brewery), banks (Bank of America Bankerettes), food companies (Balian Ice Cream Beauties), and movie companies (Columbia Pictures Starlettes). As women entered the defense industry during World War II, industrial softball and its popularity grew, and teams like those from Douglas, Calship, Perry Forge Shop, Naval Dry Docks, Shell Oil, and others joined the league.

The Amateur Softball Association (ASA) list of fast-pitch softball champions includes Hart Motors in Chicago, 1934; Cleveland's Bloomer Girls, 1935; and in the 1940s, many of the titles went to women from the Jax Maids of New Orleans. Sponsored by the Jackson Brewery, this team took national titles annually from 1942 through 1947, with the exception of 1944. Nina Korgan, the Jax Maids pitcher, was later inducted into the National Softball Hall of Fame. Before playing for the Jax, Nina had been with the Pony Express team in Missouri, and then the Higgens Midgets of Tulsa, Oklahoma. Because the ASA insisted that the athletes be amateurs, the women were employed by their companies and paid for their jobs, not for playing ball. They worked, for the most part, as filing clerks, receptionists, and typists to earn their salaries but often received incentives to reward their playing ability.

Two other Hall of Fame pitchers from the industrial leagues were Bertha Tickey and Joan Joyce, who played for the Raybestos Brakettes of Stratford, Connecticut. Tickey had a lifetime record of 162 no-hit, no-run games.

These outstanding teams were made up of women wearing uniforms that were often ridiculous. Photographs from the 1940s to 1960s show women in skimpy, silken skirts or shorts. News articles of the era often show the women playing softball, or working, or as mothers, or in traditional female activities, as the writers and photographers strove to show the feminine side of the players and thus promote their company's products.

In 1943, Philip K. Wrigley, the chewing gum company owner, decided women should be able to play professional baseball. The All-American Girls Professional Baseball League (1943–1954) is an important part of women's sports history. The best players came from the great women's softball teams. Many of the women who played on these teams are alive today, and in the 1980s they formed a League Association of former players and began holding reunions. Their archive, which is open to the public, is in South Bend, Indiana, at the Northern Indiana Historical Society.

Once again, the managers of these teams were men, which may explain why these women were always referred to as "girls." The league and the women who played for it came to public attention a few years ago through a number of television specials and movies including *A League of Their Own,* and through books, including *Girls of Summer.*

Women from fifteen to twenty-eight were listed as professional players in the All-American League. Approximately 10 percent of the players were Canadians, mainly from the province of Saskatchewan. These women were fantastic athletes. One, Dorothy "Kammie" Kamenshek, was so good she was offered (but refused) a contract from a men's professional baseball team.[6]

Although they played a long season and played hard, the women were not paid well and usually had to work during the off-season to be able to afford to play. The first woman to sign a contract for the league was Claire Schillace Donohue, who played for the Racine, Wisconsin, Belles in 1943. She made $75 a week and actually held out one year for an extra five dollars before agreeing to sign. The money was to help pay for the master's degree she was working toward during the off-season.[7]

The players were required to wear skimpy uniforms to attract attention to the game, but they were well chaperoned and were coached in charm and femininity by beauty school experts. Some of the women were married—one even pitched until her fifth month of pregnancy—some were lesbians, some were young and inexperienced, but all became sports heroes to the people of the small towns and small cities where the league teams played for twelve years.[8] The teams played mostly in the Midwest in towns of 65,000 or less. The players practiced for two to three hours a day and played more than 102 games a season for crowds of four to seven thousand spectators.[9] Now, Claire Donohue and more than five hundred other women league players have taken their places in the Baseball Hall of Fame exhibit of the All-American Girls Professional Baseball League.

MOVING INTO OTHER SPORTS

Women were becoming more and more involved in sports that had been "male only," and even the sports that seemed to be identified with rough and dirty men were being invaded by women. The Professional Women's Rodeo Association was formed in 1948, although women had been competing in barrel racing events that were held at the men's rodeo for many years.

Women who did not wish to be a part of a team were participating in sports on their own and at local YWCAs and YWHAs or other recreation groups. These women rode horses and bicycles, swam, walked, skied, hiked, played golf, and did track and field sports. As more women worked outside the home and more time-saving devices were invented, women grew more and more interested in sports and fitness. It would take another type of invention and several more years to make sportswomen a common sight and part of the everyday fabric of American life.

TELEVISION, TITLE IX, AND OTHER GREAT CHANGES

5

Amazing changes began to appear in women's sports starting in the 1950s and continuing through the 1960s and 1970s. An attitude change among physical education leaders was one of the most important changes, as it led to the development of a new women's group with the task of establishing standards for intercollegiate sports and competitions. Representatives of three groups joined together: the Division for Girls and Women's Sports of the National Association of Health, Physical Education and Recreation; the National Association for Physical Education of College Women; and the Athletic and Recreation Federation of College Women. This cooperation led to the formation of the National Joint Committee on Extramural Sports for College Women. In 1966, the Division for Girls' and Women's Sports adopted guidelines for intercollegiate sports, and the Commission for Intercollegiate Athletics for Women was formed as a supervisory body. The CIAW also took over the intercollegiate golf tournament.

Other changes included important gains for women in both amateur and professional athletics after the end of World War II. The women who had moved into the workforce during the war became role models for young women who now chose to go to college or to work. Although most young women of the post-war years still chose marriage over careers, and those who did choose careers were somewhat limited in their choices, at least the notion that women didn't have to stay in the kitchen was beginning to take hold. By the late 1960s and early 1970s, women had started knocking on boardroom doors at male-dominated corporations. The early stirrings of the modern women's movement rippled through society, and activists took up the challenge of continuing the work of the leaders who had fought for women's suffrage many years before. The sports scene kept pace with these changes and often moved ahead of the women's movement as more and more women entered the limelight in traditional women's sports and strove to make gains in sports that had previously been played only by men.

The new phenomenon of television played an important part in these changes. The invention had been demonstrated as early as 1920 with an experimental broadcast, but its actual development occurred after World War II. By 1951, coast-to-coast broadcasting was established. Entertainment programs, special events coverage, quiz shows, news, and sports contests became standard telecasts. The public was fascinated by this in-home system of entertainment, and by 1960 nearly 60 million television sets were in homes throughout the country. Stores placed television sets in their windows, and crowds gathered outside to watch favorite programs, such as Milton Berle's "Texaco Star Theater," "I Love Lucy," Ed Sullivan's "The Toast of the Town"; coverage of major news events; and regularly scheduled professional men's wrestling. When videotaping was developed in the mid-1950s, it became possible to tape sports events and air them on television at a later time. Commercial sponsors made money available for the production of sports programs— although only male sports were covered.

DECADES OF ACHIEVEMENT

Even though women's sports were rarely shown on television, female athletes were breaking barriers and setting records through the 1950s, 1960s, and 1970s. This list shows some of the barrier-breaking occurrences of these decades.[1]

1950 The Ladies Professional Golf Association received its charter.

The color barrier was broken by Althea Gibson playing in the U.S. National Tennis Championship, Forest Hills, New York.

With a new record of 13 hours and 20 minutes, Florence Chadwick became the first woman to swim both ways across the English Channel.

1952 The first Randle Women's International Team Trophy match for small-bore rifles was sponsored by the National Rifle Association and was won by the American team.

1953 Tenley Albright was the first American woman to win the world amateur figure skating championship.

Maureen Connolly of the U.S. won tennis's Grand Slam (Australian, French, American, and British titles).

1956 For the first time the College Rodeo Nationals featured a women's event—the barrel race—won by Kathleen Younger.

1957 Althea Gibson won the Wimbledon singles title and the first national clay court singles championship.

1963 The U.S. women's team won the first International Lawn Tennis Federation's Federation Cup competition.

1964 Donna Mae Mins defeated thirty-one men to become the first woman to win a Sports Car Club of America championship.

Jerrie Mock was the first woman to fly solo around the world.

1966 Roberta Gibb Bingay was the first woman to enter and finish the Boston Marathon, wearing a hooded sweatshirt so no one could identify her as a woman.

1967 Katherine Switzer openly entered the Boston Marathon and, despite objections of race officials, finished the race.

1968 Janice Lee York Romary was the first woman to carry the U.S. flag in the Olympic opening ceremony.

Kathy Kusner became the first U.S. licensed woman jockey.

1969 Sharon Sites became the first woman to sail the Pacific Ocean solo.

Cyclist Audrey McElmury won the women's world road racing championship.

Riding a horse named Cohesion, Barbara Jo Rubin became the first woman to win a race at a U.S. thoroughbred track.

1970 The Kentucky Derby had its first woman rider—Diane Crump.

Signing a contract with the Orlando Panthers to hold the ball for the point-after touchdown kicks, Pat Palinkas was the first woman to play in a professional football game.

The Virginia Slims Tennis Tournament was the first tennis tournament held just for women.

1971 Billie Jean King was the first female athlete to earn more than $100,000 in one season.

1972 Women journalists were allowed in dressing rooms in New York State to report on boxing and wrestling matches.

The Association for Intercollegiate Athletics for Women (AIAW) held its first championship.

Nina Kuscsik won the first women's competition of the Boston Marathon.

On June 23, President Nixon signed Title IX of the Higher Education Act into law, banning sex discrimination in athletics at all educational institutions receiving federal monies.

TITLE IX—A LANDMARK RULING

Title IX of the Education Act of 1972 states that no person shall on the basis of sex, be excluded from participation in, be denied the benefits of, or be subjected to discrimination under any educational programs or activities receiving federal financial assistance.

Inequalities between men's and women's programs had been so obvious and extensive that it is almost unimaginable that it took so long to enact a law to correct the situation. Before the Education Act of 1972, it was not unusual for a school to allot over one million dollars of financial aid to male athletes and nothing at all for the female athletes. In schools that did allot a women's athletic budget, that item was always the first to be cut when money was tight, while the men's budget was often untouched. Even today, male athletes are awarded $179 million more per year in scholarship money than female athletes receive.[2] So has Title IX made a difference?

Only one year before the passage of Title IX, in *Gregorio v. Board of Education of Asbury Park* (N.J.), the Superior Court of New Jersey ruled that girls *did not* have the right to join the boys' tennis team even though there was no team for girls. After Title IX, another court, this time the U.S. Court of Appeals for the 6th District of Michigan in *Morris v. Michigan Board of Education* (1973), ruled that girls *did* have the right to try out for a boys' team *even* if there was a girls' team that they could try out for and play on.[3]

Women's participation in sports on both the high school and the college level has definitely been helped by the passage of Title IX. This law requires that male and female athletes have access to equal facilities and equal benefits, including equipment, uniforms, supplies, training, practice and locker-room facilities, quality coaches and opponents, awards and banquets, and cheerleaders and bands at games.

The effects of Title IX can be seen in research as well as in the legal arena. One study shows that working women who were young enough (approximately ten years old or younger in 1972, the time of the passage of the law) to benefit from Title IX, participated in high school sports at a significantly higher rate—55 percent—than women who were in high school prior to the passage of Title IX, whose participation was only 36 percent.[4]

The United States government definitely gave women's athletics a boost with the passage of Title IX. The law forced high schools, colleges, and universities to make money available for girls' sports. This encouraged more high school girls to see sports as a source of college scholarships. This rise in participation spurred the organization of more girls' athletic teams. In 1972, there were 32,000 female track-and-field competitors; by 1989, the number had grown to 130,000 women.[5]

The fair application of Title IX in schools can be quite difficult. Do boys get to try out for girls' field hockey when there is no boys' team, as two boys from Annapolis High School did in 1986? The answer is no. Title IX sees boys as members of the over-represented sex; thus their participation on a girls' team would take away an opportunity for a girl. Boys cannot be on the girls' team. Can girls try out for the boys' team if there is no girls' team at the school in that sport? Definitely, this type of representation is permitted. Girls must be permitted to try out for a boys' team if there is no girls' team. This includes football. A coach can tell girls (or boys) that they did not make the team

*W*ith the passage of Title IX in 1972, schools and colleges began to fund girls' teams in a variety of sports. Here, a college crew team practices for a meet.

because they are too small, not fast enough, unskilled, or not up to the level of the team, but these same standards must be used to evaluate boys as well. Girls cannot be excluded due to gender.

Should the money be pooled and a school have all coed sports teams? Many people believe that football brings in revenue and should therefore be given a larger share of a university's athletic funding. This is a myth. At least 80 percent of all college football programs lose money. In 1993, two female placekickers successfully played on their high school football teams. Both played the homecoming game and were then crowned homecoming queens! As of 1995, nearly four hundred girls are playing high school football—and not just as placekickers.

The situation is still troublesome but is evolving with time.

A *high school girls' soccer game*

Nearly twenty-five years after Title IX, the number of female coaches is catching up to the number of female teams, but many girls' teams are still coached by men. This is not necessarily a bad situation, since most male coaches are every bit as good as female coaches, but more female coaches means more jobs for women. Schools are still grappling with the proportioning of money, and some have tried to solve the issue by saying that the population of the males in sports and women in sports in a school should be a determinant. For example, if 65 percent of a school's sports teams members are male, then that percentage of the budget should be allotted to them. Of course, one could argue that if more money had been allocated to women's sports, females would make up a larger percentage of the sports population and thus qualify for more money. Actually, Title IX requires proportional participation opportunities, which means the percentage of female athletes is supposed to equal the percentage of girls in the school population. This may not always work out, but it is the standard schools must show that they meet. If they cannot meet it, they must show that they are adding sports or that the sports have been offered and no other girls want to participate.

Although Title IX came too late for the baby-boom generation (babies born shortly after World War II), it was the desire of these women to be part of the sports world that fueled the drive for Title IX. There is some question as to how much Title IX affects poor women and women of color. Most reports still show these women spending the least amount of time exercising or participating in a sport.[6]

Title IX did not sail through Congress without opposition, nor was it welcomed by everyone on college campuses. Many men in charge of male athletic programs feared that the financing of women's sports programs would jeopardize the men's programs. The National Collegiate Athletic Association (NCAA) criticized Title IX even while trying to gain control of the new women's programs that would be generated by the law. The management of women's athletics fell under a new body formed in 1972 by women, the Association for Intercollegiate Athletics for Women (AIAW). The struggle for control continued for some years.

Today's women athletes have proved the positive effects of Title IX through their continued success in the sports world. Women appear on any list of well-paid sports people. Martina Navratilova, Steffi Graf, and Chris Evert are obvious examples. The results of the 1996 summer Olympics in Atlanta, Georgia, demonstrate that females can become outstanding athletes when they have access to proper training, equipment, and opportunities. The women on the U.S. Olympic team included many sensational winners and stand-out athletes. Of the forty-four gold medals awarded to Americans, nineteen were won by women, including the women's basketball, softball, gymnastics, soccer, and synchronized swimming teams. Angel Martino, Amy Van Dyken, and Amanda Beard were winners in swimming. Mia Hamm played soccer in front of seventy-six thousand fans and helped the U.S. women win. Kim Rhode, a high school senior, took the gold medal in double trapshooting. Dr. Dot Richardson had her dream come true when the U.S. women won the gold medal for softball. Kerry Strug's valiant efforts helped to put her gymnastics team over the top with a winning vault that left her injured but the team victorious. These women will now inspire more young girls to continue to demand fair funding and full opportunities.

THE STARS OF THE ERA

Before turning to the current scene, let's look at some of the barrier-breakers and record setters of the 1950s, 1960s and 1970s who became role models for millions of girls and women—even before Billie Jean King made history on television by defeating Bobby Riggs and bringing sportswomen into the twentieth century.

TENNIS

When she started playing tennis on the paved streets of New York City, Althea Gibson was not thinking about breaking the color barrier, but that is just what she accomplished. Althea took up tennis as a way to get out of her troubled neighborhood and to establish an identity for herself. She was a good enough player to attract the attention of a local recreation leader, who helped her play at an interracial tennis club. At the club, Fred Johnson, a tennis pro, offered to coach her at no charge. Dr. Hubert Eaton, a wealthy African-American doctor, took Althea to live with his

Althea Gibson, playing at Wimbledon in 1957

family and sponsored her and encouraged her to continue her studies and training. After winning all the American Tennis Association's (ATA—the African-American tennis circuit) competitions, including the 1947 national women's tournament, it seemed as if there were no more challenges for Althea. Dr. Eaton thought otherwise and helped her become the first black woman to play at the Eastern and National Indoor tournaments. However, the expected invitation for Althea to play at Forest Hills, New York, did not come. The tournament sponsor, the United States Lawn Tennis Association, was obviously not letting down its color barrier.

Alice Marble, an earlier USLTA champion, was appalled. She wrote a plea for Althea to be able to play that was published in the July issue of the *American Lawn Tennis* magazine. Challenged, the USLTA allowed Althea to play. Although she did not win in that tournament, Althea Gibson's career was a stunning one. She won the British championship at Wimbledon and the U.S. Nationals in 1957. The city of New York gave her a ticker-tape parade. Triumphant in the Nationals again in 1958, Althea also won the Associated Press Woman Athlete of the Year award. She was the first African-American woman to have this honor.

TRACK AND FIELD

At the age of twenty, Wilma Rudolph was known as the world's fastest woman. At the 1960 Olympics in Rome, Wilma won three gold medals—the 100-meter dash, the 200-meter dash, and the 400-meter relay. She was the first American woman to win three gold medals in Olympic track and field. Wilma was invited to the White House to meet President John F. Kennedy, and a parade was planned in her honor. However, she would not let the parade take place until it was agreed that it would not be segregated. Wilma was breaking gender and color barriers, and no one was stopping her.

As a young child, Wilma had suffered pneumonia and scarlet fever. For several years she was unable to walk and had to endure painful treatments and massage therapy. With the help of special shoes, she began walking again at age eight and soon made up for lost time. In high school, she excelled at basketball

*W*ilma Rudolph, in the lead at the 1960 Rome Olympics

and track and went on to Tennessee State University, where she trained under Coach Edward Temple.

Renowned for her speed, Wilma was also well-liked for her dedication and honesty and was respected for her commitment to her dreams. After the 1960 Olympics, the American track team toured Europe, and Wilma was always greeted by cheering crowds. In 1961, she was awarded the AAU Sullivan Memorial Trophy; she was the third woman in the award's twenty-five-year history to receive it. In 1995, after her death, the Women's Sports Foundation created the Wilma Rudolph Award for Courage in her honor and memory. The award is to be given to athletes who share Wilma's courage and dedication to the ethics of sports.

SKATING

Peggy Fleming was thirteen years old when a 1961 airplane crash claimed the lives of eighteen members of the U.S. figure skating team and Peggy's coach. She vowed to win in his memory, and by 1967, she was cleaning up the ice with her awards, including the North American, world, and national titles. A year later, Peggy stepped onto the ice at the winter games in Grenoble, France, and the world watched—on live television via satellite—as she skated like a ballet dancer to Tchaikovsky's "Pathétique." She won the only gold medal the United States took from those winter games. Peggy Fleming went on to win five national championships and eventually became a graceful performer on television and in ice shows.

In Denver, Colorado, Peggy's coach also worked with another young American skater, Dorothy Hamill. By age nineteen, Dorothy had held the U.S. titles in 1974 and 1975, but she was relatively unknown to the American public. That was changed when she defeated the favorites at the 1976 Olympics. She took the lead in the compulsory figure program, the first of the three figure skating requirements, which counts for 30 percent of the score. Hamill then received a perfect score of 6.0 for her short program, the second of the requirements and worth 20 percent. The third portion, the free-skating performance, worth 50 percent, was almost flawless. Skating to music from old Errol Flynn

***P**eggy Fleming, world figure-skating champion*

movies and wearing an American Beauty Rose costume, Dorothy's performance won her the gold medal. Dorothy developed a new move, the "Hamill camel," that involves a spin into a sitspin. Her hairstyle from the 1976 Olympics also started a fad as young skaters and girls all over the country copied her short haircut, which spread out like a fan when she turned or spun around. Dorothy Hamill is in the Olympic Hall of Fame.

Imagine an American three-way tie for the silver medal in speed skating! That is exactly what happened at the Olympics in France, in 1968. Jennifer Fish, Mary Meyers, and Diane Holum of the U.S. all crossed the finish line in 46.3 seconds, coming in only two-tenths of a second behind the Russian winner, Ludmilla Titova. The three-way silver was the best the U.S. had done in Olympic speed skating since it had become an event for women in 1960. The Americans bettered their record in 1972 when Diane Holum took a gold in the 1500 meters and Anne Henning won the gold for the 500 meters. A few years later, Sheila Young would win three Olympic medals for speed skating. In 1976 at Innsbruck, Austria, Sheila won the gold for the 500-meter event, silver for the 1500-meter event, and bronze in the 1000-meter event. After winning her third medal she received a call from President Gerald Ford, a fellow Michigander, to congratulate her on the honor she had earned for herself and her country.

BOWLING

On the pro bowling circuit, women were earning scores that equaled those of the men. However, the men could play in an average of one tournament a week, while the women had fewer than one a month. A top woman bowler could earn about $11,000 a year; a man could earn over $65,000.

Bowling was very popular, and weekly bowling leagues could be found in cities and towns all over the country. The top women bowlers of the 1960s and 1970s included Dorothy Fothergill, Woman Bowler of the Year in 1968 and 1969; Patty Costello, winner of the U.S. Open in 1972, who bowled an average of 205 in her prime years; Judy Cook, Bowler of the Year in 1973, with a top average of 207.2; and Paula Sperber, who in 1966 as a fifteen-year-old bowled a 290 and was Bowler of the Year in 1971. The biggest prize in bowling went to Carol Anderson, who won the Brunswick Showdown in 1975, in Las Vegas, Nevada, and received a $50,000 prize.

Because bicycling was long considered a leisure-time recreational activity, there were not many outstanding bicyclists prior to the 1970s. Twenty-three-year-old Sheila Young (of speed skating fame) changed all of that in 1973 when she won the world cycling track championship in Spain; she also won the record for the 500-meter speed skating sprint and the U.S. Amateur Bicycle League's national track championships. Sheila was the first athlete to win the world championships in both sports in one year.

Another champion cyclist, Jean Robinson, started as a cross-country runner in the early seventies. Jean was a primatologist at the University of Washington. Her particular interest in diet and training led her to competitive cycling, with as much as 35 miles (56.4 km) a day of pedaling. Her work earned rewards when she became the champion at the 1974 Women's National Road Championships in Pontiac, Michigan. Forty-five women competed in this 34.5-mile (55.5-km) event that Jean had not been expected to win, but as two accidents took out some of the riders, she pulled ahead.

Another great woman cyclist, Sue Novara, was a rival of Sheila Young in the 1970s. Novara crossed the finish line of the 1974 Match Sprint event just a half-wheel ahead of Young. In 1975, Novara won the gold at the world championships in Belgium.

Muriel Davis Grossfeld, one of the early U.S. gymnastics coaches, was herself an Olympic gymnast. Starting in 1955, Muriel took sixteen national victories in individual events before turning to coaching the United States Olympic and Pan-American teams from 1967 through 1972. Both Linda Metheny, five-time winner of the all-around national gymnastics title and winner of five gold medals in 1967, and Cathy Rigby, winner of the silver medal in World Gymnastics, were part of the U.S. team coached by Muriel.

Television had been an integral part of American life for twenty years by the time Cathy Rigby was seen on ABC's Wide World of Sports' coverage of the World Gymnastics championships in what was then Yugoslavia. Cathy began gymnastics at age eight, and soon her natural talent was so impressive that she joined the Southern California Acrobatic Team (SCAT) to work under the direction of Bud Marquette. With his guidance, Cathy devoted five years to gymnastics and developed into a first-class competitor, going with the U.S. Olympic team to Mexico City in 1968 as a fifteen-year-old. At only 4 feet 10 inches (1.47 m) and 89 pounds (40.4 kg), Cathy didn't look as if she'd be much competition for anyone, but she was spectacular and placed tenth all-around in a competition that included the fantastic Russian gymnast Olga Korbut.

Unlike most gymnasts before her, Mary Lou Retton was muscular, and her movements were more explosive than those of most competitors. In the July 1984 Los Angeles Olympics, Mary Lou won a gold medal as the all-around gymnast, silver in the vault, and bronze for the uneven bars floor exercises. She was the only woman to qualify for the finals of each apparatus event. She was named the Associated Press Woman Athlete of the Year and soon after retired from amateur competition to do sports commentary and television commercials.

GOLF

In her first full season on the Ladies Professional Golf Association (LPGA) tour, Nancy Lopez won nine tournaments and broke the record for prize money won. She is the only golfer (male or female) to be named both Rookie of the Year and Player of the Year in the same year. In 1987, she was inducted into the LPGA

***N**ancy Lopez, on the course in 1977*

Hall of Fame and two years later into the PGA/World Golf Hall of Fame. By 1991, Lopez had won over $3 million and 44 LPGA tournament victories.

BASKETBALL

Banners were waving, cheerleaders were jumping and people had paid admission fees to watch two basketball teams play at Madison Square Garden in New York City. The Mighty Macs was a team from Immaculata College in Philadelphia, and the Knightees represented Queens College in New York. It was February of 1975, and both teams were the *women's* basketball teams for those colleges! They were the leading two teams of the Association for Intercollegiate Athletics for Women (AIAW), and they proved that women's basketball was exciting for spectators. The Mighty Macs won 65–61.

One of the early great women's basketball players was Karen Logan, who played for a professional team, the Pink Panthers. Often pitted against men's teams, Karen averaged 23 points a game. She was actually drafted by the San Francisco Warriors (a men's team) in 1969, but the basketball commissioner would not allow her to play.

Developing her basketball skills in New York City playgrounds in games against girls and boys, Nancy Lieberman made it to the Olympics in 1976 and was part of the U.S. team that won a silver medal. She made the 1980 team, but the U.S. did not attend as part of the U.S. boycott of the Olympics that year. She was an outstanding shooter and ball handler and attended Old Dominion University in Virginia. In 1979 and 1980 she won many awards and was named the outstanding woman athlete of any sport by the Honda Broderick Corporation.

With offers from over two hundred colleges, Cheryl Miller was the most sought after basketball player in 1982. Her high school points totaled 3,405, and in 1983 she became the first woman to dunk a basketball during a regulation game.[7] Cheryl played on both the United States 1983 Pan-American and 1984 Olympics teams. Her awards include college-player-of-the-year Broderick Award (1984, 1985) and the Wade Trophy from the National Association of Girls and Women in Sports (1985).

Lynette Woodard of Kansas was another member of the 1980 Olympic basketball team that was unable to compete because of the U.S. boycott of the summer games. Lynette played pick-up games with her brother until her sophomore year of high school. At school, she developed her ball handling and shooting skills. The 5-foot-11-inch (1.8-m) Lynette played for the University of Kansas' Jayhawk team. She led the nation in

*L*ynette Woodard, on the court with the Harlem Globetrotters

rebounds and averaged 25.2 points per game in her freshman year. Her performances on the court and in the classroom improved each year, and she received Academic All-American honors. Her interests in college included helping to start a Big Brother-Big Sister program and volunteering for the American Cancer Society. Her efforts gained her the Woman of the Year award given by the Wichita, Kansas, NAACP.

Woodard won an array of medals, including a number of gold ones—on the U.S. women's 1979 basketball team in the World University Games; as captain of the 1982 U.S. team, which beat the Soviet Union; in 1983 at the Pan-American Games—and a silver medal at the World University Games. The 1984 U.S. Olympic Basketball team was captained by Lynette, and won the gold medal. In October of 1985, Woodard became the first woman basketball player to play for the Harlem Globetrotters, a traditionally male African-American basketball team that plays exhibition and entertainment games. After playing for the Globetrotters for two years, she left the team due to contractual disagreements. In 1986, Lynette was honored by the Women's Sports Foundation as Sportswoman of the Year.[8]

HORSE RACING

One other major professional sport attracted women in the 1970s—horse racing. Here was a sport in which they could compete directly against men and for the same money. Diane Crump became a professional jockey in 1969, and in 1973, Robyn Smith became the first woman to ride the winner in a stakes race.

AND THE SUPERSTARS

The women saved for last in this chapter have done much for the sport of tennis and for women and sports in general. In the 1970s, tennis was becoming a popular sport on television, and

*B*illie Jean King

Billie Jean King was in the right place at the right time to take advantage of the spotlight.

As a young girl, Billie Jean Moffitt enjoyed softball but turned to tennis because her father—who became her first tennis coach—felt softball was too boyish. By the age of sixteen, Billie Jean was ranked nineteenth in the nation. She got a new coach—tennis great Alice Marble—and within a year Billie Jean moved up to fourth place. She won her first Wimbledon title in 1961, the women's double (with Karen Hantze). She married Larry King in 1965 and became better known as Billie Jean King. A year later she took her first singles title at Wimbledon. King won that championship five times—in 1967, 1968, 1972, 1973, and 1975—and she won the U.S. Open four times—in 1967, 1971, 1972, and 1974. She also won the Australian Open in 1968 and the French Open in 1972.[9]

By the fall of 1971, Billie Jean King had become the first woman athlete to win $100,000 in a single year. She worked hard to promote women in sports by speaking out and demanding prize monies and endorsement opportunities more closely equal to those available to male athletes. She and her husband, who was also her manager, published a magazine for women athletes, *womenSports.* Another magazine, *Sports Illustrated,* named her Sportswoman of the Year, for the first time honoring a sportswoman rather than a sportsman.

King upheld her position as a fighter for women's rights in what was billed the "Match of the Century" and the "Battle of the Sexes" when she was challenged by the former men's national champion and self-proclaimed "male chauvinist pig," Bobby Riggs. The challenge was accepted and the date was set for September 20, 1973, at the Houston, Texas, Astrodome.

The match turned into a media event. Billie Jean presented Bobby with a pig in a pink bow, and he gave her an all-day "sucker" (lollipop). Following a parade with hundreds of musicians and people in costumes, Billie Jean was carried onto the court in an Egyptian litter while Bobby was brought in on a Chinese rickshaw. Some people expected the match would be just a funny game, but they were wrong. The players fought hard and in all seriousness. Women athletes and fans all over the world were thrilled when Billie Jean King defeated Riggs, 6–4, 6–3, 6–3.

Besides being the best of players, King was also one of the cofounders of the Virginia Slims Circuit, which was created in 1970 to increase prize money for women players. She also helped create the Women's Tennis Association, an organization that was behind the U.S. Open's awarding of equal prizes for both sexes. King was a founder of the Women's Sports Foundation and is in

*C*hris Evert

the International Tennis Hall of Fame and the International Women's Sports Hall of Fame. Billie Jean King accumulated seventy-one tournament victories.[10]

Another athlete who increased women's interest in sports was Chris Evert, daughter of tennis pro Jimmie Evert, whose whole family played the game. In eighteen years as a professional, Evert won 157 tournaments and just under $3 million. As a teenager, she had played and lost to Billie Jean King. Chris turned pro on her eighteenth birthday in 1972, and two years later she won her first two major titles, singles at Wimbledon and the French Open. From 1975 through 1978 she held the U.S. Open title and won it again in 1980 and 1982. In all, Chris had eighteen singles championships and a career record of 1,304 victories and just 146 losses. Chris Evert was the 1974 Woman Athlete of the Year and is in the International Women's Sports Hall of Fame.[11]

Born in Prague, Czechoslovakia, in 1956, Martina Navratilova began taking tennis lessons from her stepfather at age six. She won the Czech women's singles title in 1972 and came to the United States a year later. On her return to her country, she was criticized by the communist government as having become "Americanized," but they did reluctantly let her return to America for the U.S. Open in 1975. She lost in the semifinals of the U.S. Open but then defected and sought political asylum in America.

By the 1980s, Martina Navratilova had overtaken Chris Evert and was considered the best female tennis player. Some of the greatest tournament tennis ever seen was played by Chris and Martina when they competed against each other. Navratilova won at Wimbledon nine times (1990 was her last singles championship there), took the U.S. Open in 1983, 1984, 1986, and 1987, the French Open in 1982 and 1984, and the Australian Open in 1981, 1983, and 1985. The end of the 1994

*M*artina Navratilova

season was Martina's last, as she retired from the game with a record of 161 singles championships. A member of the International Women's Sports Hall of Fame, Martina Navratilova had won over $19 million by 1993.[12]

The most important success of the 1970s was the increasing opportunity for girls and women to get into organized sports, either with men or on separate teams. In 1974, girls began to play baseball in Little Leagues, although two families had to sue the organization before it would allow girls to be on teams. Colleges also increased competitive sports programs for women, and women saw sports in a new light. Many people began to support the idea that encouraging sports among young girls and helping them to develop as athletes while developing as individuals is beneficial to them and to society.

TODAY'S SCHOOL SPORTS SCENE

6

Wanting it and getting it—that's what today's sports scene is about. Striving for and accomplishing goals drives today's women athletes to train, play, and work. When Rebecca Lobo of the University of Connecticut championship basketball team was in elementary school, she wanted to play on a local team, but because only a few girls signed up she was told there wouldn't be a team. Rebecca's mother insisted that her daughter be allowed to play on the boy's team, adding that when the teams played "shirts and skins," Rebecca was to be with the shirts![1]

Young girls today have a wealth of team and sports choices in comparison to the women of their mothers' generation. As women gain more independence, so do their organizations. In 1972 in New Jersey, a twelve-year-old girl showed that she could make the cut for a Little League team. However, to prevent her from playing, the national headquarters of Little League revoked the charter for the team she had joined. Through legal battles and campaigns by groups such as the National Organization for Women, both Little League and the Soap Box Derby were soon open to girls.

Today's high school girls talk about the feeling of exhilaration and energy that they get when playing a sport. These girls often started young, by six years of age in many cases, and have developed the sense of accomplishment, teamwork, and confidence that playing sports can provide. Studies show that if a girl hasn't played a sport by the time she is ten years old, she has only a 25 percent chance of ever playing one.[2]

*T*oday schools, colleges, sports clubs, and after school leagues offer a wide range of sports activities, including field hockey, synchronized swimming, track and field, and many more.

Girls may wonder when to get involved in sports or how much time to devote to a sport. Most coaches, sports doctors, and athletes advise against pushing anyone into a sport. However, with all the possibilities that exist today for physical activity, a girl can try many sports, and then decide which, if any, she wants to stay with. Watching sports events on television or attending local high school or college games are good ways to see some of the opportunities that exist. Going with a friend to a skating rink or bowling alley, or shooting some hoops can help a young girl find out if she is interested in the sport. Watching the Olympics or figure skating specials on television with older brothers and sisters or cousins is another way to learn about the world of sports.

In talking with high school athletes who are spending the last few weeks of their summer vacation out on a soccer field, the main feeling that comes through is that these girls feel the hard work is worth it. With America's women's soccer team winning the gold in 1996, many female soccer players feel even more dedicated to their sport. These athletes don't talk about winning and losing as much as they do about being a member of the team, learning skills, building the courage to meet opponents in a tough

*S*ynchronized swimming

situation, developing the edge that makes them better at their game, learning to make quick strategy decisions, and accepting the cheers as well as admitting mistakes. Thirty years ago, the mothers of these athletes were lucky if they made the cheerleading squad. Now the mothers stand on the sidelines, season after season, in all kinds of weather, to cheer for their athlete daughters.

Being on a team teaches a girl social skills as well as athletic skills. Some of these skills can be learned elsewhere, such as in girl scouts, religious youth groups, or debate teams, but not every girl wants to be a part of these activities, and many feel the need to add sports to their activities picture. Playing a sport helps a girl (and a boy too) learn to stand up for herself and speak out for herself when necessary. Learning to be organized is another plus of sports, and athletes who learn to balance their needs with the needs of the team learn valuable lessons that can eventually pay off in the business or professional world as well. Even learning how to hang on to your position on your team when another girl challenges you can be an important lesson. An athlete may have to be a bit aggressive to hold that spot on the team, or might be forced to admit that another player is better and step aside for the good of the team. Commitment is an important issue in sports because a sports team takes so much of a girl's free time. Juggling homework and practice and other activities is not easy. Families can help by being accommodating and supportive, but a girl must manage her own responsibilities. She must also want to play for herself and not because of her family. Setting priorities is a must for any athlete. As a final note, not being afraid to take a chance during a game is something every girl should have the opportunity to learn.

GOOD COACHING

Girls' teams are sometimes viewed as having different coaching needs than boys' teams, and often girls seem to prefer a woman coach who understands the differences. For example, some people believe that girls rarely play hard against their own teammates in practice, that they save their aggression for the game; and that they learn better when the coach doesn't speak harshly to them. Girls seem to develop a closer relationship to their coaches than boys usually do. There are exceptions to this model, and generally both girls and boys look for encouragement from a coach and both want to learn to play better. Girls as much as boys like the feeling of physical strength and skill that comes from playing sports.[3]

HIGH SCHOOL OPPORTUNITIES

Besides soccer, many other kinds of sports are available to girls today. High schools, although hampered by a lack of funds, still support girls' teams in track and field, soccer, softball, basketball, field hockey, volleyball, and sometimes other sports. When schools can't afford the uniforms, teams often have fund-raisers to obtain money for uniforms or pay for them out of their own pockets. Many high schools require that team members meet a minimum grade point average, usually 2.0 with no more than one failing grade, in order to play on a team. High school clubs are also available for girls in a number of sports; many are coed, such as ski clubs, which often take several weekend trips each year. In some regions of the country, hiking clubs, aerobics, and bowling clubs are also popular.

Nearly one hundred years after its invention, basketball is a tremendously popular high school and college girls' sport. Many girls also enjoy following the college teams that are consistently in the top ten, such as the University of Texas, Penn State, Tennessee, Purdue, and the University of Connecticut. Many other sports are not as mainstream as soccer and basketball but attract their own enthusiasts. These include coed wrestling, rodeo, rhythmic gymnastics, horseback riding, and many others.

*H*urdles

Where high school teams and clubs leave off, organized leagues and recreation teams begin. In rural or suburban areas and in city neighborhoods, organized sports and pick-up games are often available for girls and boys. Soccer and basketball games on any skill level are found in nearly every city and town in the United States. Weekend league tournaments and team trips to other cities and even other countries are highlights for some of the highly skilled teams. Ice hockey is also very popular in much of the country, and many teams boast of having girl players. Players who excel in sports like soccer can even try out for Olympic development teams in the hopes of becoming proficient enough to make an Olympic team in the future. Local coaches can help a girl find out about these opportunities.

COED TEAMS

Some high schools, especially smaller schools, charter schools, and private schools, have liberal policies about students joining a team. In many cases, try-outs are not required, and students are encouraged to try a sport for a season. Due to the size of their student bodies, many small and private schools have to have coed teams in order to be able to fill the roster and to offer equal sports opportunities. Even wrestling teams are now sometimes coed, although boys on opposing teams sometimes forfeit rather than wrestle a girl.

The athletes at a small high school in Washington, D.C., have separate winning girls' and boys' soccer and basketball teams, but the wrestling team is coed, with four girls and sixteen boys on the 1995–96 team. During the season, the team trains for two hours a day, including running up and down sixteen flights of stairs at each practice. The girls and boys wrestle in their weight class regardless of gender. The coach, Sam Ross, welcomes the girls' participation, saying, " This is the second year that girls have joined the team while I've been coaching and we've done well with them. They do not train any differently than the boys. My time is spent teaching wrestling to all the players and the girls are very enthusiastic about the sport." Adding to the coach's comments, Caitlin, a second-year veteran of the team, and Wendi, new to the team this year, agree that girls train just as hard as the boys and are just as competitive and enthusiastic.[4]

As more girls develop an interest in this traditionally male sport, even public high schools have begun to field coed wrestling teams. This trend has created a bit of controversy because some male wrestlers and some male coaches feel it is wrong for teenagers of the opposite sex to wrestle each other. On the Fox television network, a recent talk show presented a panel of two male wrestlers, two male wrestling coaches, two female wrestlers, and two female football players to look at the issue of opposite sexes playing contact sports. The discussion was quite lively. The boys voiced a strong feeling that wrestling a girl is immoral and does not allow a male to treat females with respect; the boys also complained that they are laughed at if they win against a girl and severely ridiculed if they lose! The girls on the panel disagreed and stated that respect would mean treating them as sports opponents rather than focusing on their gender. These girls said that the moves in wrestling happen very quickly, and they never think of the opponent as a male but just as some- one to beat. One of the coaches on the panel agreed with the boys, one with the girls. The audience seemed to be in favor of letting girls have the opportunity to compete and stay on a con- tact-sport team if they were good enough. The two female foot- ball players talked about the rigorous "hell week" of preseason training they had to complete to make their teams, one as a kick- er and one on the field. Both play for winning high school teams. The most important comment and the logical summing up of this panel discussion came from the coach in favor of girls competing, and his sentiments apply to all sports and the rea- sons why girls as well as boys compete. He suggested that we ask ourselves why someone wants to play the sport. Does the sport build pride? Does it build character and self-esteem? Does it help a person stay in shape and be healthy? Then he simply stated, why should only boys benefit from a sport that provides "yes" answers to these questions? Girls need sports for these same reasons, and trying to keep a sport a single-sex competition is archaic.

A SPORTS SAMPLER

RODEO

When it comes to competition, few sports are as demanding as rodeo. The National High School Rodeo Association (NHSRA), with headquarters in Denver, Colorado, is a nonprofit organization dedicated to the development of good sport, fair play, horse riding skills, and character in youth. This sports association was started in 1949 by a Texas educator and rodeo contestant named Claude Mullins, and it now has a membership of over thirteen thousand students—male and female—from thirty-eight U.S. states and four Canadian provinces. The North Texas Association is another rodeo organization. At the national level of competition, rodeo contestants have an opportunity to win college scholarships totaling over $100,000 annually. Members compete at state and national levels on a circuit that runs from March to October, with the bulk of the national events taking place in June and July. During the circuit, a rodeo athlete practices for at least two hours a day and spends two to three weekends a month competing. Not only does the rodeo athlete need to be in good physical shape, but she also needs to train her horse for the events she plans to enter.

Rodeo is an expensive sport; horses, trailers, and animal food are costly, and once a person reaches the high school level the competition is difficult. But girls who ride rodeo, like Jamie McPeake of Lexington, Tennessee, say it is something they've grown up doing and hope to continue through college. Jamie started competing at age four in the junior division. Her father went to the rodeo to enter steer wrestling events, and she rode her horse around the barrel race while she waited for him. She is

*R*odeo athletes often begin competing early. Here, grade-school girls compete in a Colt Scramble at a Canadian youth rodeo.

now a high school junior who says she's "been on a horse since she was two weeks old sitting in her mother's lap."[5]

Young women, called cowgirls at the rodeo, compete in a number of events: barrel racing, which is riding a pattern around barrels, striving for a fast time; pole bending, riding in and out of pole barriers and around the end pole and back again in the shortest time possible without knocking down the poles; goat tying, similar to cowboys roping steer; breakaway roping, roping one animal in the fastest time; team roping; and cutting, taking one animal out of the herd while keeping the horse in perfect synchronized motions with the animal. Prizes are usually money or trophies or sometimes equipment such as a saddle. Jamie says that the travel is the hardest part of being in a rodeo, since there is so much to prepare and take on the road with you. Even though rodeo is a very popular spectator sport where Jamie lives, she thinks only six other girls in her high school are still competing in rodeo because the skill level is so high by that age that only the best continue the sport. When Jamie is not on the circuit, she is active in cheerleading and keeps an excellent grade point average in school. She says her involvement in rodeo does not interfere with being a teenager, but it does keep her busy. She loves it, and it is a big part of her life.

Girls as well as boys talk about the sport of rodeo as being thrilling and addicting and say that they develop a camaraderie with their animal. Most rodeo riders realize they will only ride into their twenties since competition becomes so difficult, but the benefits they feel they get from the sport seem to outweigh any risks or fears of injury. Many also say they do it hoping to win some scholarship money, as well as for the sport itself.

High school rodeo is usually a club sport, and not a varsity team, especially since students compete for money. Also, rodeo is one of the riskiest sports, and no school could manage the insurance costs. The NHSRA charges membership fees which cover insurance, and the association also certifies the rodeo arenas to be certain there is adequate medical care available for participants and to ensure humane treatment of the animals.

IN THE SADDLE

Horseback riding has been a popular sport for women for hundreds of years, and girls today love to ride as well. The sport is overwhelmingly a girls' sport, although some boys do ride and compete on national levels. This, too, is an expensive sport, with the equipment for the rider and the cost of the horse being very high. A good horse can cost $2,000 to $10,000, whether it is for dressage, combined training, show jumping, or show hunting.

On the high school level, girls usually compete in local, regional, and then national competitions. There are several big nationals throughout the country that girls must qualify for by accumulating points during the year by winning or doing well at regional contests. On the East Coast there is the Devon Horse Show, the Capital Challenge, the Pennsylvania National Horse Show, the Washington International Horse Show and the National at Madison Square Garden in New York City. In the West, the national show is the Cow Palace Grand National in San Francisco. The Midwest hosts the American Royal Horse Show in Missouri. At these nationals, and at the regional and local events, girls can win scholarships, prize money, ribbons, trophies, and coolers (blankets) for their horses with the competition's name embroidered on them. A girl who is serious about riding will practice six days a week for about two-and-a-half hours a day, including the time needed for taking care of the horse. The American Horse Show Association (AHSA) and state horse show associations oversee the sport and provide guidelines for competitions. National magazines, such as the *Chronicle*, publish articles, information, and advertisements about equestrian sports.

RHYTHMIC GYMNASTICS

A sport with less danger but great appeal is rhythmic gymnastics. This activity combines acrobatics and dancing to music. There are about one thousand girls in the nation who participate in this sport in clubs and gyms, and there is a U.S. National Rhythmic Gymnastics Team. One member of the team competed in the 1996 Olympics. The sport, which combines the beauty of dance with flexibility and coordination, was an Olympic sport until 1956 and was then brought back in 1984. An important competition for these athletes is the Rhythmic Gymnastics Challenge in Colorado Springs, Colorado, which includes competition in several categories, including hoop, ribbon, rope, clubs, and ball. Most of the gymnasts who make it to this competition have been practicing seven hours a day, six days a week, and their performances show it. Their routines are similar to the floor exercises we see in gymnastic competitions, but the athletes have the added challenge of keeping a ribbon flowing or a ball or hoop balanced as they perform their tumbling and dance routines.

As a sport, regular gymnastics is a grueling one. Petite yet strong young girls seem to be the best suited to the sport. Gymnastics takes both a physical and mental toll on young women athletes, many of whom strive hard to stay small enough to be competitive—sometimes hurting themselves in the process. Fortunately, new rules required that a gymnast had to be at least fifteen within the calendar year in order to compete in the 1996 Olympics. By the year 2000, competitors will have to be at least sixteen in that calendar year. These rules will help gymnasts stay in the sport a little longer and not put so much pressure on younger girls to eat poorly to stay small or attempt performances out of their reach and abilities. Three of the current top U.S. gymnasts are Dominique Moceanu, fourteen, winner of the U.S. Nationals Championship in 1995; Shannon Miller, eighteen, winner of the vault at the U.S. Nationals Championships; and Dominique Dawes, nineteen, winner of the uneven bars and floor exercises at the 1995 Nationals. All three were members of the 1996 U.S. Olympic Gymnastics team. This was the first U.S. team in one hundred years to win the team gold medal. The team was called the "Mag 7," and every one of the seven magnificent young athletes helped to bring home the gold. Kerri Strug strove to clinch the medal (not knowing it was already firmly in U.S. hands) with a heroic last vault that so badly bruised her ankle she had to be carried to the award platform.

An outstanding member of the Mag 7 was Dominique "Dom" Dawes, who trains in Gaithersburg, Maryland, and has many awards and distinctions to her credit. Dominique is a terrific athlete who was both the first African-American to make the U.S. Olympic Gymnastics team and the first to win the U.S. Nationals Championships (1994). At 5 feet 1 inch (1.5 m) and 102 pounds (46.3 kg), Dominique is a dedicated and committed athlete who worked hard to claim a spot on the 1996 Olympic team.

In a recent interview for this book, Dominique Dawes reminisced about how she began in gymnastics at age six. She feels she was motivated to stick with the sport because she liked it, and she also came to enjoy the chance to travel and to meet people. Now Dom trains five to eight hours a day, six days a week, and says that maybe the long hours involve some sacrifice. However, she doesn't feel that her sport interfered with her teenage years. Dom graduated from high school in 1995 and was the homecoming queen at her school. She took classes at the University of Maryland for a year while training for the Olympics.

"We have practice from six to nine in the morning, and then I go to school till two o'clock, and then practice from six to eight or nine at night," Dom explained. She has traveled throughout the U.S. and several other countries. Dom is not sure what career she will eventually pursue, but she plans to enter Stanford University and says she is interested in studying criminology. She plans to stay active in her sport by helping out with exhibitions and working with younger gymnasts.

Dom's advice to young girls interested in gymnastics is "to believe in themselves, to set goals, and to make sure they are happy with what they are doing. Be motivated, have determination, dedication, and perseverance to keep going."

Dawes feels that gymnastics has been changing and points out that the judges are more knowledgeable about the sport and that the rules change every four years. As gymnasts become more and more proficient, skills are downgraded. More is required for the compulsory exercises, and a gymnast has to do

Dominque Dawes performs at the 1996 Olympics.

more for a good score. Thus, the level of competition keeps rising. She also feels that the officials and coaches now know much more about nutrition and the needs of girls' bodies, which has been very helpful for the athletes in developing better stamina. She doesn't feel that she has had to diet, other than sticking to low-fat foods, nor has she seen other girls starving themselves or using drugs of any kind.

When asked if she saw herself as a role model, Dom replied, "I guess sometimes I do see myself as a role model for young girl athletes. I want to tell them to remember that education comes first, and an education lasts forever. It's good to have other hobbies and athletics on the side, too. Growing up, I had people around me whose character influenced me and helped me. Gymnastics takes a lot of hard work, and I haven't done it alone. I've had help from my coaches, my friends, my family, and my teachers. We all worked together and produced the happiness in me."[6]

WOMEN OF THE HOOPS

Another happy group of athletes is the 1996 U.S. national women's basketball team, from whose members the Olympic team was formed. They were coached by Stanford University's Tara Van Derveer, and the women made sacrifices to be on the team. Some sacrificed financially, by leaving high paying positions on European teams, others sacrificed by leaving husbands, children, and jobs or even delaying weddings and medical school to spend the year training and playing a schedule that took the women on an international tour. U.S. fans were excited about the University of Connecticut's win in the NCAA championships and perfect season record. Rebecca Lobo, the 1995 College Player of the Year, has helped to increase the popularity of women's basketball among fans. Other players on the U.S. team included Jennifer Azzi, Ruthie Bolton, Lisa Leslie,

Nikki McCray, Carla McGhee, Dawn Staley, Katy Steding, and Sheryl Swoops. Sheryl signed a contract for a major commercial endorsement, and following the pattern set by some male athletes, she will have sneakers designed for her that will be named "Swoops."

As a standout player, Rebecca Lobo has advice about nutrition for athletes. Talking about her eating habits while training, she mentions that eating right and drinking lots of water are high priorities. Foods that are a high source of carbohydrates such as pasta, and chicken for protein, are good choices. These foods help give an athlete energy before a game. For snacks, she recommends bagels and fruit, for both their nutritional value and ease of carrying along on a bus or plane. She also emphasizes eating breakfast every day and being sure to replenish with water when exercising.[7]

SPORTS CAN TAKE YOU TO COLLEGE

College athletics have boomed in this generation, and more money is available for scholarships than ever before. However, there are more girls competing for money and positions than there are money and positions. There were over ten thousand scholarships at eight hundred colleges and universities available in 1994, but far more than ten thousand athletes were vying for the offers. Here are a few suggestions from the Women's Sports Foundation on how to maximize your chances of making it to college on a scholarship, and also pointers on which sports are getting the money.

Start early to look at schools and let schools look at you. Choose several schools that are within your reach in the areas of cost, athletic level, and scholastic requirements. Visit the schools and meet the coaches; bring a video of yourself and a team schedule so the coach will be able to scout you in an actual game situation. Be realistic about the goals you set—can you be a scholastic success at this school and can you get enough financial support? If not, work on a plan for another school. Ask questions when you visit the school to find out if there is a faculty athletics committee, what the graduation rate is for athletes, how many athletes graduate in four years, whether there are career counseling opportunities, if tutors are available to athletes, and whether the faculty is responsive to the needs of athletes who must sometimes miss class for games.

Also look into daily life at the schools you visit. Find out what conference the school is in and how the team has performed in recent years. Learn how much practice is involved and how long the season is and investigate the coach's basic philosophy. Try to determine the student body's reception of athletes and how well athletes and non-athletes mix during the school year. Ask what happens to the scholarship if you are injured and whether the college will ask you to sign a letter of intent (saying you will attend the school) with an offer of a scholarship. It is also important to know what the grade requirements are for keeping the scholarship and if you can participate in more than one sport a year.

From Alabama State University to the University of Wyoming and all the thousands of colleges between, you can find some of the following sports and some scholarships offered for female athletes: archery, badminton, basketball, bowling, crew, cross-country, fencing, field hockey, golf, gymnastics, ice hockey, lacrosse, riding, riflery, rodeo, sailing, skiing, soccer, softball, swimming and diving, synchronized swimming, tennis, track and field, and volleyball.[8] Start early to work with your high school guidance counselor or a college consultant to improve your acceptance chances. With family support and some hard work and effort, you have a good chance of finding a scholarship or other financial aid to help you in college.

WOMEN'S SPORTS COME TO TELEVISION

Finally, the Olympics of the early 1990s featuring Kristi Yamaguchi and Nancy Kerrigan convinced television programmers of the large viewing audience eager to watch the sport of figure skating and, perhaps, other women's sports. Now, instead of waiting four years for the next Olympic competition on TV, American viewers are treated to excellent televised competitions every few months. Spooky figure skating specials are even telecast for Halloween! This interest in figure skating has helped to create a giant industry as girls (and boys) all over the country dream of Olympic gold as they leap and spiral through practice sessions on the ice. Some of the high-school-age competitors lighting up the ice are Nicole Bobek, who was crowned champion at the 1995 Nationals, and Michelle Kwan, who is only fourteen but is already the U.S. National Champion. The United States Figure Skating Association (USFSA) and the International Skating Union have mixed feelings about this boom in coverage of figure skating. On the one hand it is terrific to have so many opportunities for the athletes. However, so many of these telecasts are promoted by people outside of the guiding organizations that the traditional rules are often ignored. Both organizations realize that more opportunities to win money are important for athletes, who have tremendous training costs. The leaders of the USFSA point out that these telecasts are entertaining, but it is the USFSA that contributes to the development of the amateur skaters through the funds they raise from private and corporate contributors.[9]

Opportunities for women in sports have never been greater. Whether you participate as a high school student for the fun and prestige of it, or work hard to use sports to get to college, the experiences you derive from your involvement in sports can never be taken away from you, and you will recognize the changes and improvement in yourself. Whether you win or lose, make it to the pros or help your high school team get a trophy, the experience of participating in a sport can and should make you feel happy.

CHILLS, THRILLS, AND SUPERSTARS

7

When Nancy Kerrigan and Kristi Yamaguchi came to town for a World Professional Figure Skating Championship, the reporters and fans turned out in huge numbers to see these popular superstars. Cameras and media people were everywhere, and every word the stars said was taken down and recorded. This is the world of the professional athlete. The rewards are tremendous, both Nancy and Kristi are financially comfortable women, and the $50,000 prize for the championship is just a portion of the money each earns for appearance fees and endorsements. These are two of the most admired of America's Olympic figure skaters, and two of the lucky ones who have won medals, money, and fame.

Getting to that pinnacle is not easy. Many athletes reach the peak of their careers at such a young age that the fame and money can become too difficult to handle. We often read or hear about super college athletes who realize their dream of making it to the pros only to overdose on drugs at a celebration party before ever playing a professional game. Young male football, baseball, and basketball players are sometimes pushed onto a fast track—going from being a college junior or senior to a professional twenty-one-year-old making a hundred thousand dollars a year or more, and being surrounded by reporters and fans. The superstar effects can be dizzying, and it takes a level head and the support of family, friends, coaches, and good advisers to help the athlete weather the storm of fame and carve out a long professional career.

Women who make it to the world of professional sports have to struggle with the headlines as well, although few professional sportswomen take home the huge amounts paid to male pros. As one example, the Colorado Silver Bullets baseball team is a terrific professional women's team. This team does a good job of playing against men's pro and college baseball teams for six months of the year. The women players earn much lower salaries than do the men they compete against.

The negatives that accompany star status in professional sports may be a loss of privacy and also a feeling that the sport you have loved for so long is now just your work and career. Some athletes keep their wits about them and their love of the sport alive by spending time with young athletes who are struggling up the ladder and need the role models that the professionals have become. When Nancy Kerrigan was at the December 9, 1995 World Professional Figure Skating Championships in Landover, Maryland, she talked about how inspired she was by the young girls competing in the U.S. Figure Skating Association's eastern sectional championships and how working with younger girls on the ice helped her keep motivated and excited about skating.[1]

ON THE WAY TO STAR STATUS

For young ice skaters, arriving at a sectional championship can seem like a dream come true. To reach this level in amateur sports is exciting, and many young athletes who get there have spent ten or more years practicing and competing, and often spending as much as $30,000 a year for travel, coaches, ice time, and equipment. They look up to the professionals and yearn to make it to the national championships and then the next level and the next until they finally become professionals, too. From amateur to professional in any sport is a long road, and many decide along the way that a piece of the dream is enough. In reality, their love of the sport may outweigh their talent. Many choose to accept their medals and triumphs and move on with their lives, some into coaching or sports-related careers and others into entirely different fields. But most athletes, whether they become pros or not, will agree that the efforts they expended as amateurs were worth it and that they have learned about and lived a life that was worth the pressures of the competitions, the financial costs, and the injuries and sacrifices that often accompany a sports career.

In ice skating and in other sports, female superstars were rare until our era. Now we see women in sports that reflect the way society's attitudes have changed. Women have changed also. These changes started in the 1970s, as women began to become visible on athletic fields and in every other sports area across the country and began to break other sports barriers. Laura Blears Ching competed against men in surfing in 1973; Phyllis Ackerman was the first woman to do sports commentary for a professional basketball team, the Indiana Pacers, in 1974; Janet Guthrie was the first woman to drive in the Indianapolis 500 auto race, in 1977; Eva Shain was the first woman to judge a world heavyweight fight, in 1977; and Mary Driscoll Shane was the first woman to do play-by-play broadcasts of baseball games, in 1977.

Today, women are participating in many "thrill" sports, those rugged sports requiring endurance and even having an element of danger. Women have taken to activities such as car, horse, and motorcycle racing, the martial arts (including kick-boxing), windsurfing, parachuting, skydiving, long-distance running, bike racing, snowboarding, white-water rafting, kayaking, water skiing, rock climbing, orienteering (using a map and compass to complete a course through the woods), luge, and even surfing.

THE PUBLIC CHEERS FOR ATHLETES

Not everyone can be a superstar, but Americans love to watch them, read about them, and buy the products they endorse. In the last decade, many professional women athletes and Olympians have achieved superstar status and yet have remained focused and true to their sport, and are generous in helping younger athletes. Selecting a few of these women to represent female athletes was not an easy task; each one however, *is* a fascinating superstar.

One sport that is "chilling" just to think about is the Alaskan Iditarod Trail Sled Dog Race, a 1,161-mile (1,868.4-km) race that has been won by women five times. Libby Riddles was the first woman to win, and after six years of not competing, she was back for the 1995 race, although she did not win it.

The Iditarod is a marathon race that dates back to the earliest known inhabitants of the region, the Ingaliks, a group of the Athabascan Indians who settled the interior of Alaska. They lived in villages along the Yukon River, subsisting mainly on salmon. They also traveled inland to hunt caribou in a place they called Haiditarod, meaning "the distant place." By 1908, one of the last gold strikes was found in Alaska, and miners established a town on the site of the native caribou hunting grounds, spelling it Iditarod. The Alaska Road Commission, at the urging of the miners, marked out a trail, which was originally called the Seward Trail, for a race. The Seward Trail covered what is now the interior portion of the marathon; however, the marathon was eventually extended until it covered more of Alaska and was renamed the Iditarod.

A good, strong dog team is vital to a successful run at the Iditarod. Most teams consist of seven to eighteen dogs; they run in pairs with the lead dogs as the "brains" of the team. The lead dogs take the commands for *gee* (right) and *haw* (left); they keep the team on the trail; and they use their sense of smell when the trail can't be seen due to snow and wind. The driver stands in position about 40 feet (12.2 m) behind the lead dogs.

*L*ibby Riddles, first woman to win the Alaskan Iditarod Trail Sled Dog Race, with her sled-dog leaders.

The Iditarod crosses much of Alaska, passing through different climate systems and changing land forms. Starting in Anchorage, the trail leads through spruce and birch forests, across frozen lakes, and along rivers. The temperatures are a bit warmer here, with winds blowing from the Pacific Ocean. The trail travels on through the mountains, rising up to Rainy Pass, 3,200 feet (975.4 m), and then out of the mountains and down into colder and icy climates of 30 or even 50 degrees Fahrenheit below zero (−34.4°C to −45.5°C). Going through the tundra, the trail reaches the Yukon, with its frigid temperatures and winds of 50 miles an hour (80.4 km/h). When the trail drops to the coast of the Bering Sea, another climate is encountered as the Arctic weather is slightly warmed by winds off the water. The trail reaches toward Nome, where the winds are so severe they can knock over the dogs and sled.[2]

The minimum equipment required for the race includes an Arctic sleeping bag, ax, snowshoes, two sets of booties for each dog, at least two pounds of food per day per dog, and a day's food for the person who is the racer (musher). Most of the drivers know they need more than these basics. Officials check each entrant's supplies before the race starts. They usually take a dog-food cooker, a cooler for the food, feeding pans, sled repairing tools, spare lines and harnesses, head lamps and batteries, compass and topographical maps, firearms (in case of a wild animal attack on the dogs), and personal items. With the driver included, a sled packed for the Iditarod weighs between 3 and 5 hundred pounds (136 to 226.8 kg). The dogs are eager runners who together pull all this weight at a speed of 11 to 12 miles an hour (17.7 to 19.3 km/h). Drivers need approximately sixty-five hundred calories a day for the grueling race, and they tend to prefer foods that provide high energy—pizza, steaks with pats of butter, and fried chicken. Libby Riddles also took along peanut butter sandwiches, French toast, fruit juices, dried moose meat, cake, popcorn, yogurt, and ice cream. Teased about her junk food, she admitted that she enjoyed looking forward to what she'd eat at the next checkpoint.[3]

Libby Riddles headed for the adventures and snowy wilderness of Alaska at the age of sixteen. She had a love of animals that made her interest in sled racing natural, and she eventually entered the Iditarod race from Anchorage to Nome. She won the Iditarod in 1985 and was also named the Pro Sportswoman of the Year by the Women's Sports Foundation. Articles about her appeared in *Sports Illustrated* and *Vogue* magazines and she was awarded the humanitarian award given by the Iditarod veterinarians to the driver who has taken the best care of her or his dogs during the race.

The Iditarod winner from 1986 through 1988 and again in 1990 was Susan Butcher, who modestly says she only coached the dogs, they did all the work. In 1990, Butcher set a record of 11 days, 1 hour, 53 minutes, and 23 seconds.[4]

Butcher, like Riddles, preferred the outdoors to city life, and after leaving school she moved to Colorado, where she met and worked with a woman who bred and raced sled dogs. Reading about the 1973 run of the Iditarod, Susan decided that was her goal and soon moved to Alaska to train her dog team. She lived in a small log cabin and hunted for her food, chopped wood for heat, and hauled her own water. She entered her first Iditarod in 1978; she finished nineteenth, but a year later she had moved up to ninth. She then trained for six years, traveling up to 7,000 miles (11,265.4 km) a year. In 1985, she was on her way to a possible win when a moose killed two of her dogs and injured thirteen of the other dog-team members. She dropped out and watched Libby Riddles become the first woman winner. Butcher lost her chance to hold that distinction, but she is credited with being the woman to win the most times. Her other awards include the Professional Sportswoman of the Year, given by the Women's Sports Foundation (WSF), for 1987 and 1988; Outstanding Female Athlete of the World in 1989, given by the International Academy of Sports; and a World Trophy award given by the Amateur Athletic Foundation in 1990.

Lisa Anderson's teenage years in Florida were difficult, and she spent many of her days in surf shops or out surfing to get away from her troubles. At age sixteen she left home, heading for the surf of California, and now, ten years later, she is the number one female surfer in the world. Happily, Anderson has also reconciled with her family. In 1994, she took the first women's pro champ surfing title since 1988, and she hopes to win it again this year. Anderson is twenty-six years old, 5 feet 7 inches (1.7 m) tall, and weighs 123 pounds (55.8 kg). She has been a member of the Association of Surfing Professionals World Tour since 1987. Since joining the tour, she has competed and won all over the world. Anderson has been told she surfs like a man, but this young mother, the first woman surfer on the tour, may actually be better than many of the men surfing today.[6]

One of the best jockeys in horse racing, regardless of gender, is Julie Krone, winner of the 1993 Belmont Stakes on a horse named Colonial Affair. The Belmont is one of the triple crown races, and Krone was the first woman to win one of these three important races.

Julie Krone started as an equestrian rider (one who takes a horse through jumps), but by the age of thirteen she had determined to be a great jockey. Starting her career as a groom, she soon rose to exercise rider and then jockey. Her first win was at Tampa Bay Downs in 1983, and then from 1987 to 1989 she was consistently among the top five jockeys in the nation. She was the top woman jockey in the nation in 1983 and also from 1986 through 1993. Before an ankle fracture, broken finger, and pierced elbow from a fall took her out of the 1993 season, Krone

*L*isa Anderson, a surfer, rides a wave.

had accumulated a career total of 2,300 wins and over $30 million in earnings.

Riding in the 1995 Kentucky Derby, Krone was the fifth woman to do so and was thought to have a better chance of winning than any of the women who had participated before. Patricia Cooksey rode *So Vague* to an eleventh place finish in 1984, Krone placed fourteenth in 1992, Diane Crump was fifteenth in 1970, and Andrea Seefeldt finished sixteenth in 1991. Krone is petite, just 4 feet, 10½ inches (1.5 m) tall and weighing just 100 pounds (45.4 kg); she is also vivacious, witty and determined. Her second time at the Derby, she rode *Suave Prospect.*

The 1995 Derby winner was not Krone's horse; it was

Thunder Gulch. Krone did not win the record nor the roses of the winner's circle, but she did finish eleventh, which was her best run, and she tied the women's top accomplishments at the Kentucky Derby.[7]

England's Queen Victoria is responsible for the existence of an 8-pound (3.6 kg) silver ewer known as the America's Cup. In 1851, the queen awarded this prize to an American team in a sailing race, and it has been called the America's Cup ever since, regardless of which country wins the race.

The winner of the 1992 Cup was William Koch, and he wanted to put some spark back into a 144-year-old race that seemed to be drawing less attention and fewer fans. He thought an all-female crew would pique spectator interest in the race. Women had been part of previous teams, but an all-female team had yet to be tested on a 25-ton (22.7-metric-ton) boat with a 3,400 square-foot (315.9-sq-m) sail.

Koch set about to recruit and outfit a women's team. As an heir to an oil fortune, he was personally able to contribute five million dollars, a fourth of the women's budget. This partial budget would pay to hire coaches, fund-raising experts, trainers, and some other personnel. Koch also gave the team his two best yachts as training vessels, and a great deal of technological equipment to help them be up-to-date for the race.

Six hundred and seventy-eight women thought William Koch had a good idea and came to the tryouts for the team. Included in those hoping to make the team were Olympic athletes; experienced sailors, including two women who had sailed through hurricane force winds in another race; weightlifters; aerospace engineers; and three women who were mothers of small children. All hoped for one of the twenty-nine team positions of which only sixteen are allowed to sail the boat during the race. Some of the women selected were team navigator Annie

America 3 *crew members work their craft during the America's Cup competition.*

Nelson, Linda Lindquist, and Dawn Riley. The crew of the *America 3,* or *Cubed* as the boat was called, knew they were considered underdogs, and they occasionally had to deal with hostile anti-women jeers and comments.

Finishing second to Australia in the International World Championships off San Diego, California, the women earned attention as well as respect. Television specials, news interviews, and articles followed the team and their run to the finals, where they lost by seconds. One member of the crew said the race wasn't a "battle of the sexes. This is about having fun. And about winning."[8]

Another "thrill" sport women enjoy is bike racing. Race Across America Marathon (RAAM) is an annual, coast-to-coast bike race that starts in Irvine, California, and finishes in Savannah, Georgia. Seana Hogan is one of the endurance cyclists who puts herself to the test in this grueling race. The winner of the 1994 RAAM, Seana lived on a 10,000-calorie-a-day liquid diet during the race, but she still experienced dehydration and had to stop in Tennessee for intravenous rehydration. After four-hours' rest, she was off again to complete the 2,905-mile (4,674-km) competition. She was determined both to win for her third time and set a women's record for the race time. She crossed the finish line in nine days, eight hours, and fifty-six minutes, breaking the old record for the women's transcontinental race.

Hogan began riding in 1991. While recovering from a divorce, she took up riding to clear her head and began riding to work, 40 miles (64.4 km) round trip, and riding during lunch. Now, from January to April she trains 450 miles (724.1 km) a week and in May, as the RAAM nears, Hogan ups that to 600 miles (965.4 km). With a master's degree in mathematics, Hogan often performs mental calculations while racing, comparing her speed and distance to previous races and other racers. As a single mother of a young son, Hogan says she could never do what she does without the help of family and friends.

Jane Quigley, a track cycling racer, and Jeanne Golay, a 110-kilometer road racer, are two other "thrilling" women who are athletes in the growing sport of women's cycling. Jane started when she was just fourteen and recovering from a soccer knee injury. Now at age twenty-five, she studies nutrition and dietetics at the University of Wilmington, Delaware, and is a four-time national champion in the individual-pursuit race. In this race, two cyclists start at opposite ends of the track and try to beat their opponent's time.

Jeanne Golay was the top U.S. cycling finisher at the 1992

Olympic Games in Barcelona, Spain, with a sixth-place finish. Golay used to live in her car and travel to races to win whatever prize money was available, and that wasn't very much. Over the past several years, women's cycling has grown, and she is now a member of the Saturn cycling team and is sponsored by Trek, which has allowed her to move into a home and continue training and winning.[9]

WINNING WOMEN

Today's winning superstar women are found in many sports, both indoor and outdoor, winter and summer. You recognize their faces and names immediately, and many of them continue to help young female athletes who want to learn and grow as they compete. Some of these women are Olympic winners, some are now professionals, and some are both. A few superstar favorites of young adult fans are Bonnie Blair, Monica Seles, Jackie Joyner-Kersee, Florence Griffith-Joyner, Kristi Yamaguchi, Picabo Street, and Janet Evans. Others you may not know as much about are Grete Waitz and Sherry Potter-Cervi.

SPEED SKATING

The biggest group of fans for speed skater Bonnie Blair is her own family, known as the "Blair Bunch." They have happily attended every one of her important competitions and cheered wildly for Bonnie at the Olympics. Born in Cornwall, New York, Bonnie began Olympic-style speed-skating at the age of sixteen. This style of skating involves two skaters on the track who race against time but not each other. By 1982, Bonnie was good enough to compete in Europe, but she didn't have the money to make the trip. Her neighbors and friends, with the organizing assistance of the police department in Champaign, Illinois, where she was living, raised the necessary money through raffles and bake sales.

*S*peed skater Bonnie Blair

Over the next several years, Blair steadily moved up in competition, taking the indoor U.S. speed-skating title in 1983, 1984, and 1986. She was the North American indoor champion in 1985, and in 1987, she set a world record of 39.43 seconds in the 500-meter event of the world competition. She set another record at the 1988 Olympics and won the gold in the 500-meter. The 1992 Olympics brought Bonnie to the attention of Americans who didn't know much about speed skating, and they watched enthralled as she won gold for both the 500-meter and the 1000-meter, becoming the first skater to win two consecutive golds for the 500-meter. She received the Sullivan Award as the nation's outstanding amateur athlete that year and has continued to be a speed skating star. As the Blair bunch went wild in the stands at the 1994 Olympics, Bonnie won two gold medals. Named the 1994 and 1995 Sportswoman of the Year by the Women's Sports Foundation, Bonnie then retired from competition but not from the sports world. She plans to help new athletes and further the cause of women in athletic endeavors.

TERROR ON THE TENNIS COURT

Sitting on a bench at a tournament in Germany, Monica Seles, a top U.S. tennis player, was attacked by a fan of her chief competitor, Steffi Graf. The fan stabbed Monica in the back with a nine-inch (22.9 cm) knife, so as to disable her and let his favorite win. This 1993 injury was expected to keep Seles out of play for a month, however, her anxieties were so great that she did not come back until the Canadian Open in 1995.

Born in Yugoslavia in 1973, Monica started tennis at a young age and was taught by her father. It was his instruction that created her unusual and powerful two-handed forehand and backhand. While still a young teen, she went to the Bollettieri Tennis Academy in Florida, where her aggressive style and her talent made the other girls refuse to practice with her; so she was matched against the boys, including the young Andre Agassi. In 1987, Seles turned professional and won the French Open singles and in the next few years continued to win seven out of nine other singles tournaments, including the Australian Open and the U.S. Open in 1991. Seles became the best female player in the world and is now, after her recovery, back in top form and on the tennis circuit again, which makes fans and other athletes very happy. Her fight to overcome her fears and regain her competitive edge have inspired other women and athletes in general.

ON TRACK

Jackie Joyner, the five-time gold medalist, played volleyball and basketball in high school, and after graduating in the top 10 percent of her class, she attended the University of California on a basketball scholarship. She also worked with coach Bob Kersee on the seven-event heptathlon (two days of events, including the long jump, 100-meter hurdles, shot put, high jump, 200-meter run, javelin throw, and 800-meter run) and by 1983 had won the Broderick Award as the nation's top female track-and-field athlete. Qualifying for the 1984 U.S. Olympics team in the broad jump and the heptathlon, she didn't do as well as expected due to a hamstring injury. Marrying her coach in 1986, she added Kersee to her name and, with his skillful coaching, continued to add to her performance in the heptathlon and the individual events. At the 1986 Goodwill Games in the former Soviet Union, she became the first woman to score more than seven thousand points in the heptathlon and was that same year named the Athlete of the Year by *Track and Field News*. She also received the Jesse Owens Award and the Sullivan Memorial Trophy. Joyner-Kersee competed in the high hurdles and long jump throughout 1987, and at the world championships she won both the pentathlon and the long jump and was the first woman to win an individual and multi-event at such a high level of competition. The Women's Sports Foundation named her the 1987 Amateur

*J*ackie Joyner-Kersee prepares to throw the javelin in a heptathlon event.

Athlete of the Year. Winning in the 1988 and 1992 Olympics, she became the first woman to win multi-event titles at two Olympics and the first athlete (of either gender) to win medals for multi-event competitions in three Olympics. Sadly, the 1995 Atlanta games were probably the farewell Olympic competition for Jackie Joyner-Kersee. Injured and pushing her limits of strength and endurance, she withdrew from the heptathlon and competed only in the long jump, winning a bronze.

Atlanta saw many other American women do well in track-

and-field competitions. Gail Deevers won a gold medal and is considered the fastest woman today. Gwen Torrence won bronze in the same 100-meter dash. Together, they were two of the four women who won gold in a relay race.

Shattering the previous world record in the women's 100-meter dash in 1988, Florence "FloJo" Griffith-Joyner was called the world's fastest woman. Catching the eyes of sports fans with her tremendous speed, long fingernails, and glitzy race outfits, FloJo won three golds and a silver in the Seoul, South Korea, Olympics of 1988. In the 100-meters, her world record of 10.49 seconds was outstanding.

Growing up in a poor section of Los Angeles, California, Florence ran track and competed in the Sugar Ray Robinson Youth Foundation, a program for underprivileged youngsters. Later, while in high school, she ran track and set school records for the long jump and sprinting. Financial difficulties made her leave college after one year, but Bob Kersee, coaching at UCLA, convinced her to enroll at his school and specialize in the 200-meter race. Barely missing a spot on the 1982 Olympic team, Florence worked hard at the World Class Track Club in Los Angeles, training with Kersee for the 1984 Olympics. Although she won the silver medal in the 200-meters, she decided to retire from sports. Three years later, she rejoined the World Class Track Club and set up a rigorous training schedule that included weightlifting. Florence had decided to see if she could run better or if she should stay retired. During this time she met and married Al Joyner, a former Olympic triple-jump gold medalist and the brother of Jackie Joyner-Kersee. In 1988, at the U.S. Olympic trials, her training efforts paid off when she won the 200-meter and then took three golds at the Olympics in individual sprints, the 400-meter relay, 200-meter relay, and a silver in the 1,600-meter relay. FloJo was named Female Athlete of the Year by the

Associated Press and also won the Sullivan Award as the nation's outstanding amateur athlete. Soon after, she retired and began designing and modeling the type of clothes that had made her a stunning looking as well as outstanding athlete.

ON THE ICE

Only 5 feet (1.5 m) tall and weighing about 90 pounds (40.8 kg), Kristi Yamaguchi combines athleticism, grace, and style with great skating skills. In 1992, she won the national, the world, and the Olympic championships, and although she was expected to go to the 1994 Olympics, she turned professional instead. Apparently, Kristi is enjoying herself as an entertainer more than as a competitor, and skating fans are happy to see her on the ice.

SKIING

A favorite of the fans in the 1994 Olympics, Picabo Street is a whiz on the ski slopes. The daughter of "free spirit" parents, Picabo was named for a town in which they lived and because she liked to play peek-a-boo as a small baby. In December of 1995, Street tied for third place in the World Cup downhill race in St. Anton, Austria. She shared third with an Austrian skier, and that country took first and second place as well. This win put Street at the top of the downhill standings for the U.S. and looking good for future wins.

SWIMMING

America's first female Olympic swimming champion and the only person to win all the women's swimming events at a single Olympics (1920) was Ethelda Bleibtrey. She later said that the pools were so unsuitable it was like swimming in mud. She won every race she entered from 1920 to 1922. In 1919, she broke the rules at a New York beach by taking off her stockings and was given a ticket for swimming nude—despite being otherwise fully clad in a swimming outfit of the times! The publicity from this

P*icabo Street aloft during a downhill run*

action caused the law to be changed so that women could thereafter swim without stockings.

More modern swimming stars include Janet Evans, who dominated the 1987 U.S. Championships with her wins in the 400-, 800-, and 1,500-meter freestyle and the 400-meter individual medley. The first woman to break the sixteen minute time for the 1,500-meters, she also stood out in the 1988 Seoul Olympics with gold medals in the 400-meter and 800-meter freestyle events and the 400-meter individual medley. Evans set the world record of 4:03:85 in the 400-meter freestyle. She went on to win seven national championships, the Sullivan Award, and world championships. She also swam for Stanford University, winning awards for her school as well. At the 1992 Olympics, she won gold in the 800-meter freestyle and a silver in the 400-meter.[10]

The 1996 Olympics produced many winning women, including Amy Van Dyken, the first U.S. woman to win four gold medals in one Olympic season.

RODEO

Sherry Potter-Cervi, riding on either of her horses, *Trouble* or *Hawk,* is at the top of the barrel racing competitions for women in the Women's Professional Rodeo Association. She has won more money than any woman on the circuit and also more than any of the men! Her earnings of over $125,000 are remarkable, and she is only twenty years old. Recently married, Sherry lives in Arizona and spends a large part of the year riding the rodeo circuit, something she has done for most of her life. Another rodeo champion from 1994 and 1995 is Kristie Peterson. She rides a great horse, named *Bozo,* that cost only $400—a great bargain, since most good barrel-racing horses cost four or five times that amount![11]

RUNNING

As a twenty-five-year-old teacher, wearing her hair in pigtails, Grete Waitz lined up for the 1978 New York City Marathon. She was the first woman to cross the finish line—her time, two hours, thirty-two minutes, and thirty seconds. By 1992, Grete had won the New York City Marathon nine times, beaten her own record, and set a world record, as well as participating in three Olympics and setting six world records. Starting as a world-class track runner, Grete decided to try the New York City Marathon and lined up with the 9,835 other runners for her first try. There was no stopping her after that. Due in great part to her efforts, women were included in marathon running in the 1984 Olympics.

A native of Norway, Waitz is the first and only athlete to be awarded her country's prestigious St. Olaf medal, and Norway has created a marathon, the Grete Waitz Run, for women only, in her honor. In 1995, forty-three thousand women participated in this marathon, and Grete Waitz was there to see it and cheer them on. Grete Waitz was inducted into the International Sports Women's Hall of Fame in 1995 and still continues to work with runners and with young people to encourage them to become involved in sports.[12]

Joan Benoit, a marathon runner in the 1984 Olympic Games, ran the 26.2-mile (42.2-km) race in 2 hours, 24 minutes and 52 seconds. This great record proved that women belong in modern marathon racing, and helped to establish women in this sport.

PARALYMPICS

Winning is what Sarah Reinertsen wants to keep doing. She is a student at George Washington University in Washington, D.C., and she also set the 100-meter world record of 19.38 seconds in Barcelona, Spain, in 1992. Sarah, who sprinted to the finish, is an above-the-knee amputee and was competing in the National Wheelchair and Amputee Championships. Sarah hoped to be in the August 1996 Paralympics, held after the Olympics, but her events were not held because of a lack of participants.

Competitors at the Paralympics participate in events for people who are blind or are dwarfs, for amputees and for those with cerebral palsy, and for wheelchair users and people with other disabilities. Unlike the Special Olympics, these games are for participants who are serious, elite athletes, and many were world-class athletes prior to becoming disabled. One participant, Joyce Luncher, now attending the Catholic University of America in Washington, D.C., was born without a right forearm and hand, yet she holds four United States records for disabled swimmers.

These athletes and their competitions are getting to be very popular—four thousand athletes from 115 countries competed in the 1996 games. The main corporate sponsor for the 1996 competitions was Home Depot, but other companies, such as IBM, United Airlines, and Coca-Cola have also contributed. ESPN airs a program, called *Break Away,* that features disabled athletes and their sports, and the magazine *Sports 'n Spokes* shows these competitors for the superb athletes they are.

A few universities recruit disabled athletes, most notably the University of Illinois and the University of Texas at Arlington. Linda Mastrandreea of the University of Illinois has cerebral palsy and first learned about the wheelchair races when she started college. She points out that there are forty-nine million disabled, and with a population that size, she feels disabled sports and events should be drawing more attention and more fans. Opportunities are increasing at a slow pace, but these athletes are achieving recognition and setting records.

SPECIAL OLYMPICS

The Special Olympics is an organized athletic competition on local, national, and international levels for youth and adults with mental retardation. Entrants in the Special Olympics include more than one million participants from the United States and over one hundred foreign countries. Created in 1968, Special Olympics includes competition in aquatics, basketball, track and field, ice skating, wheelchair events, volleyball, tennis, softball, golf, team handball, and table tennis, and demonstration sports such as powerlifting.

Whether as local players or as professional stars, women athletes are improving their lives through sports. Nearly four thousand women competed in the 1996 Olympics, and hundreds more were coaches. As women athletes leave the playing

*S*ports offer rewards for enthusiasts at every level of ability—beginners, stars, people with disabilities, and others. Here, a runner prepares to pass the baton at the Special Olympics.

fields and begin sports-related careers, they will search for new physical challenges and competitions and maintain their skills. Sports offer women many career paths, as athletes, coaches, promoters, agents, and in a variety of other sports-related professions.

PROBLEMS AND POSSIBILITIES

8

*A*nger and shock are the emotions most people feel when they hear the story of the girls' basketball team from Oglala, South Dakota. The team was participating in the YMCA Quad State tournament held in Rapid City, South Dakota, when the coach was told his team of girls would be disqualified because they had a boy on the team! The coach was amazed and learned that the accusation had come from a team his girls had defeated in a tournament earlier that month. No one authorized the search, but nonetheless, a YMCA volunteer took the entire girls' basketball team into a locker room where each girl was required to show the waistband of her panties and her bra straps! The search was made without the coach's consent, but the girls would not have been allowed to play if the search was not completed. The team was sent a letter of apology from the director of the YMCA; now the coach plans to take birth certificates with the team to future tournaments.[1]

Questioning the gender of women athletes has been a sore point for as long as women have been competing in athletic events. Babe Didrikson was accused of being very "manly," and so have other women who excelled and appeared to be too good at a sport to be women. Men have long held the idea that males are superior in sports to any woman, yet most people know men who can be beaten by women in many sports. Female athletes have had to endure strip searches, extensive questioning, and other humiliating experiences in order to compete in sports.

Although this type of abusive behavior seems to be lessening as officials and the sports world become more sensitive to fair play, the girls from South Dakota know it still happens far too frequently to be ignored. Even in the 1996 Olympics, women were required to take gender tests to rule out the possibility of men pretending to be women to compete in women's events.

EATING DISORDERS

Girls who participate in gymnastics are also beginning to know that there are abuses that should no longer be ignored. For years now, gymnasts have been more successful if they keep their bodies small and light in weight so they can perform the amazing leaps and balancing routines that are required to win in this sport. Cathy Rigby, who led the 1972 U.S. Olympic Gymnastics team to a fourth-place finish, is now speaking out on the hazards of such gymnastic practices. She wants to see young girls participate as long as possible and with as little emphasis on weight limitation as possible. Through her years in the sport, Rigby saw girls who suffered from anorexia nervosa and bulimia in their efforts to remain thin.

Anorexia is a condition characterized by self-starvation and a drastic loss in weight, a preoccupation with food and caloric intake, the wearing of baggy clothes or multiple layers of clothing to cover up weight reduction, mood swings, and the avoidance of social situations where food will be consumed. Bulimia, also a disease mostly of females, is characterized by binge-and-purge eating habits, excessive concern about weight, bathroom visits after eating to vomit (purge the body of food), depressive moods, and being overly critical of one's body. These conditions are both serious, even occasionally fatal, and the help of a medical professional and counseling may be needed to overcome either disorder. Concern about the hazards of extreme emphasis on size and physical appearance and the improved knowledge of nutrition are helping to bring a sounder approach to the sport of gymnastics today.

STEROIDS

The abuse of drugs to gain an advantage in training or competition is another area of concern today. Although women have not been accused or found guilty of using anabolic steroids nearly as often as men have, some abuses do exist. Anabolic steroid use is banned in every sport, and its use is always secret and illegal. Some athletes, however, risk it for the short-term benefits they believe the drugs will give them. Steroids may help an athlete train longer and harder and recover from strenuous exercise more quickly than nonusers. Most athletes who abuse steroids tell themselves that using them for several years over a sports career will not be a problem, but legal risks (including being banned from competition) aside, serious medical risks do exist. The most notable of these are deterioration of internal organs and uncontrollable aggressiveness. In addition, women face the risk of becoming more masculine-looking and creating serious hormonal problems for their bodies. Teenagers may suffer drastically if they abuse anabolic steroids. The abuse can cause stunting of growth, increase of blood pressure, liver damage, infertility, and other effects.

The use of steroids in sports has existed for as long as twenty years, and Olympic records set by steroid users have been voided when steroids were detected. One of the first instances was in 1977, when East Germany's Ilona Slupianek, a shot putter, was caught using steroids.[2]

As we have become more aware of the disastrous side effects of steroid use, most athletes have tried to stay away from the drug. Yet many women athletes talk about the pressures of competing in a society that applauds and rewards victories and the setting of new records. These athletes also worry about competing against other women who may still use the drugs. Even though detection techniques have become quite sensitive, steroid use still occurs at championship events such as the Olympics.

SEX TESTING

Sex testing could be done through the same urine test used to detect steroid abuse, yet women are still subjected to other medical tests to be certain that a male is not competing in a female category. Men are not subjected to this insulting invasion, but women are subjected to the Barr body test or the polymerase chain reaction test to determine femaleness. Both of these tests have often resulted in false identification of women as men, or too male-like, and athletes have been forced to face disgrace or fake an injury so as not to compete once they failed the detection testing.

In 1993, the International Amateur Athletic Federation (IAAF) recommended that gender verification tests be abolished. The IAAF findings included the information that there is currently no evidence that men are pretending to be women in competitions and that the urine test for steroids would show any "fake" females. The International Olympic Committee still believes that the tests are necessary to avoid scandals.[3]

ADVANCES AND NEW OPPORTUNITIES

Despite abuses and scandals, we need to remember that women are making definite advances in sports. They are playing in a wide range of activities, including many that were once closed to them. They are encouraged (or at least allowed) to enter local, national, and international competitions. They are also beginning to find professional and business opportunities.

Even if we never watch a sports telecast or read a book, newspaper, or news magazine about sports, we could find evidence of women's advances in sports by looking in the neighborhood video store. Usually placed in the family section, or in some enlightened stores, in the sports section, exercise videos by women far outnumber those made by men. Richard Simmons, a weight and fitness entrepreneur, still turns out videos such as "Sweatin' to the Oldies," but his videotapes are almost lost among the many dozens of those by women.

Hollywood is often credited with the start of the exercise video with Jane Fonda being one of the first to make a video extolling the benefits of staying fit and healthy. Now videotapes are available by Cindy Crawford, Cher, Marilu Henner, and Elle Macpherson, to name just a few. Athletes are also producing videos for the fitness market, and a viewer can work out, via video, with FloJo, Donna Richardson (national aerobics champion), Rachel McLish (world women's body-building champion and Ms. Olympia), or Cory Everson (a six-time Ms. Olympia). These videos cover every possible exercise variety from toning and stretching to fat burning and yoga. Special videotapes are made for exercising the whole body or just buns, abs, or thighs. You can dancercize, do calisthenics, step-aerobics, and low- or high-impact aerobics with a video as your guide.

Without leaving one's home, a viewer can turn to ESPN's *Getting Fit Program* and *Body Shaping,* as well as fitness programs produced for many early morning network telecasts. These videotapes and television programs have become a big business and provide additional career opportunities for many women athletes. The women who watch and use them have also benefited greatly as they become more fit and develop an interest in an area of sports and physical fitness that has helped make American women healthier and more conscious of the need for exercise.

Before the videotapes, before all the television coverage of gymnastics and figure skating, before Billie Jean King, few women had a sports byline in a newspaper. The women's movement and women athletes helped bring about a change in the way women were able to cover sports events. Finally, women who loved sports and knew sports were getting a chance to interview athletes and report on sporting events. One of the first to report sports was Lesley Visser. Writing on assignment for the *Boston Globe* newspaper, she waited outside a locker room for football player Terry Bradshaw, only to have him emerge and autograph the pad she was holding for her interview notes! Visser has laughed about her early years of reporting sports, especially football, saying it was "like being a foreign correspondent" because she was a female in the land of men.[4]

Visser persevered and eventually covered football games with Bradshaw and saw more women enter the workforce as sportswriters and broadcasters. Some of the women writers who broke the barriers for today's women include Betty Cuniberti, Mary Garber, Jane Leavy, and Lynn Zinser. Few women in sportswriting today are much past their forties because hardly any women were writing about sports more than twenty years ago. It is a viable career choice for women today as more television coverage of so many varieties of sports makes sports broadcasting a good field for women.

Sports, now a sixty-billion-dollar-a-year industry, has grown to be bigger than the automobile, oil, lumber, and air transportation industries. Many universities offer degrees in fields such as sports psychology, exercise science, and sports nutrition. Even sports management degrees are available in many colleges. Women have finally broken into many sports areas previously dominated by men, and also have served as the chief medical officer of the U.S. Olympic Committee, as members of the International Olympic Committee, as president of an NBA club, and as president of the NCAA.

Television networks are responding to the changes in society by including more women as part of sports-coverage teams, and many women provide commentary on the sidelines of football and basketball games, interviewing players before and after the games, and even anchoring the sports desk for the nightly news.

Until recently, Christine McKendry's business card read, "Sports Anchor, WJLA-TV, Washington, D.C." As a weekend sports desk anchor, Chris also covered stories during the week and was often on camera in the studio or on a sports field covering events for this ABC affiliate station. In an interview with McKendry she spoke very candidly about her job, the skills women need for sports broadcasting, and how much she enjoys her terrific career.

On Saturdays and Sundays, Chris sat at the news desk at six and eleven P.M., delivering the highlights of the day's sports. Weekdays, she was a sports reporter covering the day's sports events or working on a feature story about sports. The hours changed every day as did the sports events she covered. One day the assignment might be professional hockey, on the next, basketball, and on the next a grade school sporting event. She covered it all, from kids to pros, as long as it was sports related. The main anchor, Rene Knott, took the material Chris gathered as a reporter and put it into the news show when he anchored the sports desk on weekday nights. Chris has recently moved into a new job with ESPN, the cable sports network.

Chris credits playing a lot of sports while growing up, such as soccer, basketball, tennis, and swimming, with helping her to do her job. Her three brothers, and then a college tennis scholarship, kept alive her involvement with sports. Chris says that even though she grew up surrounded by and knowing sports, she didn't think about the field as a possible career until she began a college internship in broadcast news. Chatting at the water cool-

Women with an interest in sports often enjoy sports-related careers. Chris McKendry is a SportsCenter anchor with ESPN, a cable sports network.

er or with employees of the station, Chris always knew the sports information and amazed her coworkers with her knowledge. They encouraged her to think about sportscasting rather than news. But being a sports fan isn't enough to carry this job, Chris says. There is a great deal of homework involved, and she has learned as she works, but she emphasizes that sportscasting is not as easy as it looks on TV. Names and numbers are always changing, and you have to keep up with the information. The workload is not easy and the hours make dating and seeing family a bit tough, but if you like sports and television, it is a great way to make a living.

Chris stresses that it isn't necessary to be an athlete to do her job, but liking sports and knowing sports are essential to doing the job well. She makes the point of telling girls that it isn't vital to be the star player on a team; the manager and the person who keeps the statistics are also an integral part of the team, and girls can feel they are making a contribution in these positions as well. Starting early to know about sports is key for success in sportscasting. It is also important to improve these skills:

Getting along with people—you deal with everyone from million dollar athletes to five-year-old fans.
Writing well—strong writing helps your work and words stand out.
Liking sports—enjoying your work is essential to doing a good job in sports reporting.

The number of women in sportscasting is very small, but it is growing. Chris notes that although she was the first woman in Washington, D.C., to have an anchor position on weekends, she is no longer the only woman sportscaster when she covers a sports event. Chris thinks most major cities have at least one woman on the sportscasting team of each major network, and now when she goes to a game she sees a lot of women there. Women no longer have to deal with being the only female in the room! She has heard horror stories from women who have been in the sportswriting business longer than she and who were often the only woman in a large crowd of male reporters and had to be extremely aggressive to get a story.

A high school athlete sent a question along with me to my interview with McKendry. She wanted to know if male athletes resented female reporters. Chris thought carefully and then said that she had never been harassed or hassled in any way by male athletes. She feels that such attitudes and actions are a thing of the past and that athletes have changed with the times. Athletes are business people now, and public relations and their personal images are very important to them and to their teams. Not staying in the locker room after asking her questions is one way Chris says she shows the athletes her respect, and she appreciates their respect in return. She doesn't "buddy-up" to the male athletes the way some male reporters are able to, but at the same time she feels she can become friends with the female athletes in a way male reporters might not be able to. Basically, Chris says, these things tend to work themselves out, and gender doesn't become an issue in her job.

McKendry spoke about the costs of fame to women athletes, and she expressed the feeling that the privacy factor is probably the biggest issue. Since there aren't a great many professional teams for women, fewer women than men are going to be recognized on the streets. Still, privacy is often lost. Yet, as Chris points out, her life is perhaps similar to the lives of pro athletes, and she takes the good with the bad. Some lack of privacy is balanced by the benefits of being in a big city, being around great athletes, viewing sporting events, and being well rewarded for her work. Women athletes today know what they are getting into. They have made conscious choices and if they begin winning the medals and events, they expect the glare of the spotlight along with the glory of the job.

Lack of privacy may be a negative in Chris' s job, but it is not the only one. Again she compares the negatives in her career with those faced by professional athletes: moving away from her family to get a start in the business, long hours, night hours, and few weekends off. On the other hand, Chris feels that being the best in any field requires sacrifices, and sports people are not alone in working hard to get ahead. "People find my job fascinating for two weeks, novel for one week, and absolutely dreadful after that!" she laughs.

Women are still not doing much play-by-play reporting of sports events and Chris thinks that is the next barrier to be broken. A few women are doing women's and men's basketball games play-by-play, so the field is a growth career area for women. The Association of Women in Sports Media is a professional organization for women who work in sports broadcasting, and it strives to reach young women in college who may be aspiring writers or broadcasters.

Finally, Chris suggests that girls interested in her type of career should, first, work on writing skills in high school. She advises that girls work on the school newspaper covering games, write the sports portion of the yearbook, interview the coaches, and also watch sports on TV. Generally, she suggests that girls should develop a portfolio while still in high school and then choose a college with a school or department of communications. Next, while in college, they should try to get internships with a television station or newspaper to get hands-on experience. Finally, they should be very positive about themselves; being an elite athlete is not the only way to a sports career, and writing and speaking skills are important tools for a sports broadcasting career. Chris emphasizes that the sports field is one in which lucky breaks are very important, so you need to be around and working extra hard when someone is ready to hire a new person. In the field of sports, as everywhere, it helps to be a capable woman.[5]

FAST CARS AND FAST COMPANIES

One very capable woman who has moved back and forth between the race car tracks and the corporate world is Lyn St. James. Named "Rookie of the Year" in 1984, a year later Lyn became the first woman to exceed 200 miles per hour (321.8 km/h). She has participated in and won many races as a single driver or partnered with others, and in 1992 she became the second woman to qualify for the Indy 500. Lyn St. James has also been a consumer advisor to Ford Motor Company, an ESPN and Showtime commentator, and in 1990, she was the first active athlete to be elected president of the Women's Sports Foundation. She is also the author of a book, is a columnist, and has her own sales and marketing firm.

The family business of manufacturing football equipment was a long way from her first career choice of teaching music, but Julie Nimmons is indeed the president of Schutt Manufacturing Company. The face masks you see Emmitt Smith, Steve Young, and other players wear are made by her company. In fact, every player in the Superbowl will wear a face protector made by Julie's company. Recently, the Schutt Company has moved from helmets and face masks into the production of equipment for other sports. When her family watches football games, they look for their company's products and cheer for the teams they supply.[7]

COACHING AND TEACHING

Many capable women have been quietly succeeding in the sports world as coaches. One fine example is Jody Conradt of the University of Texas "Lady Long Horns." Conradt is the winningest coach

Skills developed on a sports team may often help in a career choice.

in women's basketball, with a record of 654 wins and 178 losses. Ninety percent of her players graduate, and she has recently been inducted into the Women's Sports Foundation's Hall of Fame.[6] The University of Maryland in College Park also has a terrific women's basketball team, coached by Ms. Chris Weller, who is credited with more than four hundred wins. The director of athletics at the University of Maryland is Debbie Yow, one of the first female athletic directors at a U.S. university or college.

A career in the educational field remains an excellent opportunity for women, given the number of jobs available and the ease of obtaining them. The earning range for teachers is lower than in some of the other fields; however, the shorter hours leave time for coaching or for your own athletic activities.

Many sports careers are now open to women. Young women should think about futures in sports-related fields if they find their interests and talents included in the chart that follows.

SPORTS RELATED CAREERS

Be a pro athlete on a
soccer, volleyball, golf, basketball, gymnastics, swimming, skating, racing, or bowling team.

Work with a pro team as a
team, business, or equipment manager; marketing or public relations expert; secretary, athlete's agent, accountant, publicist, or lawyer.

Communicate about sports as a
journalist, sportscaster, writer, TV or radio broadcaster, announcer, photographer, videographer, or cameraperson.

Sell sports as a
sporting-goods store manager or salesperson, manufacturer's representative, or souvenir dealer.

Coach, officiate, or support sports teams as a
coach, college sports director, fund raiser, physical education instructor, camp director or counselor, umpire, referee, judge, or lifeguard.

Keep athletes healthy as a

sports medicine doctor, psychiatrist, psychologist, physical therapist, fitness expert, health club manager or instructor, or personal trainer.

LOOKING AHEAD

Where are women headed in the sports future? This is a challenging question, and a number of issues need to be addressed as women continue entering sports careers. These issues include the fact that while many athletes are African-American, the representation of women of color in coaching and administration is low. Studies estimate that only 5 percent of physical education teachers, coaches, or administrators are minority group members.[8]

Equity in sports must continue to improve. Women have moved into many fields and must continue to do so, especially since sports coaching is an area of continued inequity. Although U.S. universities and colleges are now producing some of the finest athletes in the world, professional teams for women need to be developed in America. As of now, most of our athletes who want to play on professional teams travel to northern Europe, Italy, Japan, and New Zealand. With the success of the women's Olympic basketball team, a pro league may be started in the U.S.

Twenty years ago, a career for a woman in sports was rare. Today the field is increasingly open, but women still do not have a fair share. It is up to women to strive for equity through mentoring programs for young women, by taking legal actions using existing laws, by lobbying sports businesses, and by supporting female athletic events. We need to continue to seek a role for women in sports off the playing fields as well as on them.

Young girls interested in sports careers should set career goals and write to the appropriate professional organizations for advice and information about school and career opportunities.

Talking with school counselors will help girls construct a program to meet their goals. Following a plan of action will help girls to reach careers in sports-related fields. This generation of young women should help even up the numbers so we see more women in sports businesses and more women breaking both sports records and gender barriers. Hopefully, one day soon, the sports pages of newspapers will devote half their coverage to women's sports and 50 percent of the teams' coaches will be women. Professional teams for women will be common, and women will own many of the professional teams. Mothers and daughters will cheer for female ice hockey teams, and no one will need to submit to a gender test! We have the skills, we have the young women with the dreams, and we have the chance to make it all happen. Just ask any woman in sports, and she will probably tell you, succeeding in sports takes hard work, some sacrifice, and lots of luck.

Good luck to every young female athlete or fan; find your dream and work for it. We're cheering for you.

NOTES

CHAPTER 1

1 *Sports Illustrated for Kids* (December 1994), pp. 42–43.
2 *Sixteenth Annual Women's Sports Award Gala,* Women's Sports Foundation and Turner Broadcasting Network, October 1995.
3 *Fair Play?* Women's Sports Foundation, East Meadow, N.Y., 1995

CHAPTER 2

1 Reet Howell, ed., *Her Story in Sport* (West Point, N.Y.: Leisure Press, 1982), p. 52.
2 Howell, *Her Story in Sport,* pp. 19–31.
3 Howell, *Her Story in Sport,* p. 48.
4 Howell, *Her Story in Sport,* pp. 122–126.
5 Gipe, George, *The Great American Sports Book* (New York: Doubleday, 1978), pp. 331–332.

CHAPTER 3

1 Alan Guttman, *Women's Sports, A History.* (New York: Columbia University Press, 1991), p. 112.
2 Phyllis J. Read, and Bernard L. Witlieb, *The Book of Women's Firsts* (New York: Random House, 1992), pp. 41–42.
3 American Journey, "History in Your Hands: Women in America," CD-ROM Series. (Connecticut: Primary Source Media, 1995), Topic: Sports.
4 Geoffrey Ward, *Baseball Who Invented the Game?* (New York: Alfred A. Knopf, 1994), pp. 6–9.
5 Reet Howell, *Her Story in Sport* (West Point, N.Y.: Leisure Press, 1982), pp. 8–121.
6 Howell, *Her Story in Sport,* pp. 127–129.
7 Guttman, *Women's Sports, A History,* pp. 163–164.

CHAPTER 4

1 Reet Howell, *Her Story in Sport* (West Point, N.Y.: Leisure Press, 1982), p. 314.

2 Allen Guttman, *Women's Sport, A History* (New York: Columbia University Press, 1991), p. 144.

3 Janet Woolum, *Outstanding Women Athletes: Who They Are and How They Influenced Sports in America* (Arizona: Oryx Press, 1992), p. 26.

4 Howell, *Her Story in Sport*, p. 112.

5 Amateur Athletic Union, "Basketball Committee Report," Minutes of the Amateur Athletic Union. (New York: Amateur Athletic Union, 1930), p. 196.

6 Lois Browne, *Girls of Summer: In Their Own League* (Toronto: Harper Collins, 1992), p. 5.

7 Tracy L. Glisson, "In a League of Her Own" (Potomac, Maryland *Gazette,* June 15, 1994) p. A–10.

8 Browne, *Girls of Summer: In Their Own League,* pp. 6–7.

9 Glisson, "In a League of Her Own," p. 7.

CHAPTER 5

1 Janet Woolum, *Outstanding Women Athletes: Who They Are and How They Influenced Sports in America* (Arizona: Oryx Press, 1992), pp. 27–29; *Sixteenth Annual Women's Sports Award Gala,* Women's Sports Foundation and Turner Broadcasting Network, October 1995.

2 *Sixteenth Annual Women's Sports Award Gala,* Women's Sports Foundation and Turner Broadcasting Network, October 1995.

3 Alan Guttman, *Women's Sports, A History* (New York: Columbia University Press, 1991), p. 221.

4 *Sports and Fitness in the Lives of Working Women* (New York: Women's Sports Foundation and *Working Woman* magazine, 1993), p. 2.

5 Sally B. Donnelly, "Work That Body!" *Time* (November 8, 1990), p. 68.

6 Donnelly, "Work That Body!", p. 68.

7 Woolum, *Outstanding Women Athletes,* p. 155.

8 Bert Rosenthal, Lynette Woodard, *The First Female Globetrotter* (Chicago: Children's Press, 1986), p. 45.

9 Hickok, Ralph. *A Who's Who of Sports Champions: Their Stories and Records.* (Boston: Houghton Mifflin Company, 1995), pg 437–438.

10 Hickok, *A Who's Who of Sports Champions,* pp. 437–438.

11 Hickok, *A Who's Who of Sports Champions,* pp. 233, 437–438.

12 Hickok, *A Who's Who of Sports Champions,* pp. 437–438, 587.

CHAPTER 6

1 *Sixteenth Annual Women's Sports Award Gala,* Women's Sports Foundation and Turner Broadcasting Network, October 1995.

2 Walt Harrington, "Step Up or Step Back," *The Washington Post* magazine (November 26, 1995), pp. 16–20, 30–37.

3 Michael O'Shea and Haskell Cohen, "Meet *Parade's* All-America High School Girls Soccer Team," *Washington Post Parade* magazine (March 5, 1995), p. 9.

4 Interview with coach and team, Edmund Burke School, Washington, D.C., December 7, 1995.

5 Interview with Jamie McPeake, Lexington, Tennessee, November 27, 1995.

6 Interview with Dominique Dawes, Gaithersburg, Maryland, October 26, 1995.

7 "Reebok Nutrition Tips from Champs, Rebecca Lobo," *SportsTalk, the Women's Sports Foundation Newsletter for Young Athletes* (Summer, 1995), p. 6.

8 "Scholarship Guide," Women's Sports Foundation, 1995–96.

9 Martha Duffy, "Crowded Ice," *Time,* (February 27, 1995), pp. 67–70.

CHAPTER 7

1 Christine Brennan, "A Thin-Ice Union of Dreams," *Washington Post* (December 9, 1995), pp. D1, D3.

2 Riddles and Jones, *Race Across Alaska: First Woman to Win the Iditarod Tells Her Story* (Harrisburg, Pa.: Stackpole Books, 1988), pp. 10–15, 124–125.

3 Riddles and Jones, *Race Across Alaska,* pp. 64–65.

4 Ralph Hickok, *A Who's Who of Sports Champions: Their Stories and Records* (Boston: Houghton Mifflin, 1995), p. 111.

5 "Fanfare," *Washington Post,* (March 5, 1995), p. D2.

6 Franz Lidz, "Mother on Board," *Sports Illustrated* (November 13, 1995).

7 Interview, Communications Office of Churchill Downs, Kentucky, December 12, 1995.

8 Margot Hornblower, "Will They Blow the Men Down?" *Time* (January 16, 1995), pp. 66–67.

9   Jane Gottesman, "A Pair of Pedal Pushers," *Women's Sport + Fitness* (October, 1995), pp. 30.

10 Kay Milles, *From Pocahontas to Power Suits* (New York: Plume Books, 1995), pp. 157–158.

11 Kenneth Springer, "Viva Las Vegas," *Women's Pro Rodeo News* (December 1, 1995) volume 27, number 12, pp. 10–11.

12 *Sixteenth Annual Women's Sports Award Gala,* Women's Sports Foundation and Turner Broadcasting Network, October 1995.

CHAPTER 8

1   "Fanfare," *The Washington Post* (December 24, 1995), p. D2.

2   Alan Guttman, *Women's Sports, A History* (New York: Columbia University Press, 1991), pp. 255–256.

3   Mariah Burton Nelson, *The Stronger Women Get, the More Men Love Football: Sexism and the American Culture of Sports* (New York: Harcourt Brace & Company, 1994), pp. 72–76.

4   Interview with Lesley Visser, ABC Television Network, December 31, 1995.

5   Interview with Christine McKendry, WJLA–TV, Washington, D.C., May 18, 1995.

6   *Sixteenth Annual Women's Sports Award Gala,* Women's Sports Foundation and Turner Broadcasting Network, October 1995.

7   Interview with Julie Nimmons, ABC Television Network, December 31, 1995.

8   "Career Packet," Women's Sports Foundation, 1992, pp. 2–5.

FOR MORE INFORMATION

Blais, Madeline. *In These Girls, Hope Is a Muscle.* New York: Atlantic Monthly Press, 1995.

Browne, Lois. *Girls of Summer: In Their Own League.* Toronto: HarperCollins, 1992.

Cahn, Susan K. *Coming on Strong: Gender and Sexuality in Twentieth Century Women's Sport.* New York: Macmillan (The Free Press), 1994.

Costa, D. Margaret, and Sharon Guthrie. *Women and Sport: Interdisciplinary Perspectives.* Champaign, Ill.: Human Kinetics, 1994.

Goldstein, Margaret J., and Jennifer Larson. *Jackie Joyner Kersee: Superwoman.* Minneapolis: Lerner Publications, 1994.

Grace and Glory: A Century of Women in the Olympics. Chicago: Multimedia Partners and Triumph Books, 1996.

Hart, Philip S. *Flying Free.* Minneapolis: Lerner Publications, 1992.

Hickok, Ralph. *A Who's Who of Sports Champions: Their Stories and Records.* Boston: Houghton Mifflin, 1995.

Karlin, Len. *The Guide to Careers in Sports.* New York: E. M. Guild, 1995.

Knudson, R. R. *Zanbanger.* New York: Harper & Row, 1977.

Lee, George L. *Interesting Athletes: Black American Sports Heroes.* New York: Ballantine Books, 1990.

Milles, Kay. *From Pocahontas to Power Suits.* New York: Plume Books, 1995.

Nelson, Mariah Burton. *The Stronger Women Get, the More Men Love Football: Sexism and the American Culture of Sports.* New York: Harcourt Brace, 1994.

Page, James. *Black Olympic Medalists.* Colorado: Libraries Unlimited, 1991.

Porter, A. P. *Zina Garrison, ACE.* Minneapolis: Lerner Publications, 1991.

Rapoport, Ron, ed. *A Kind of Grace: A Treasury of Sportswriting by Women.* Berkeley, Calif.: Zenobia Press, 1994.

Riddles, Libby and Tim Jones. *Race Across Alaska: First Woman to Win the Iditarod Tells Her Story.* Harrisburg, Pa.: Stackpole Books, 1988.

Ryan, Joan. *Little Girls in Pretty Boxes: The Making and Breaking of Elite Gymnasts and Figure Skaters.* New York: Doubleday, 1995.

Scholarship Guide, 1995–96, Women's Sports Foundation and Ocean Spray. Women's Sports Foundation, Eisenhower Park, East Meadow, N.Y., 11554.

Woolum, Janet. *Outstanding Women Athletes.* Arizona: Oryx Press, 1992.

Young, Perry Deane. *Lesbians and Gays and Sports.* New York: Chelsea House, 1994.

Internet Resources:
http://www.lifetimetv.com/WoSport
http://www.feminist.org/research/sports5.htm
AOL keyword WSF

INDEX